Final Arrangements

Final Arrangements is a story of friendship. It's also a work of my imagination. I was inspired by the city I know and love and, of course, the most wonderful garden club in the world, but in no way did I attempt to recreate any person, place, or thing.

Thank you to those who read and re-read *Final Arrangements*. Bill, Jolynne, Carol, Becky, and Marona, what you did and did not say kept me going.

To my family, I love you and thank you for your sacrifice and constant encouragement.

Final Arrangements is dedicated to my mother, who is able to leap tall buildings in a single bound. Her tombstone, though it's probably already bought, etched, and paid for, should read:

A Godly Woman

A Lover of Family

Her Bed Was Always Made

—Diane

I planted, oh, so carefully,
A pretty Little Willow Tree,
Then stuck a stick beside the tree
To see how fast it grew for me.
I'm not ashamed
To say I cried,
When the darn stick grew,
And the Willow died.

—Author Unknown

1998 HILLCREST HEIGHTS GARDEN CLUB

Founded 1955

Office	Member (Daughter)
President	Mona (Sheralyn)
Treasurer	Claire (Gina)
Horticulture	SueBee (Helen)
Parliamentarian	Charlotte (Brooke)
Flower Show Co-Chair	Mona & Claire
Sunshine & Cloudy Weather	Louise

CHAPTER 1

Pretending to be vulnerable was *such* an effort, like holding one's breath underwater while wearing a black negligee. It was almost midnight and the woman at the bar had been at Jackson's for almost three hours, balancing herself on a chrome-legged stool that had a cracked leather seat and wobbled when she moved. She would have left earlier, but that would be like quitting and quitting was a whole lot worse than pretending to be vulnerable.

Gina Sessions casually let her head loll to one side, then the other, so that her thick black hair moved in slow motion. Cat-like, she stretched herself, rolled back her shoulders, then lengthened her neck and counted to three. A quick check in the mirror over the bar told her no one had noticed, so she deflated and allowed herself a few moments to chase the slivers of ice around and around in her glass.

When they had melted, Gina pretended to smooth her lipstick in the mirror and focused on a huddled group of men at a table behind her. They made an interesting picture, like *Dogs Playing Poker*, splayed across chairs and hunched over breeding beer bottles. She hid a yawn, then swallowed the last of her watered down drink.

A sharp sound of scraping wood got her attention. It came from the table as two from the group attempted to walk toward her. They stumbled, kicking and dragging empty chairs, and as they drew closer, Gina dropped her eyes and carefully pushed her glass away from the edge of the counter. No one noticed she squared off her shoulders to the bar and tightened her neck muscles.

The alpha male was built like the Grand Canyon, deep and wide. He walked with a swagger and his cirrhosis-of-the-liver-looking belly hung over a belt buckle big enough to serve a small salad. The smaller one was in a pitiful state from either too much cold medicine or too much beer. She also noticed his weepy eyes and the red handkerchief he held to his nose. Their sport coats and ties looked like they'd been wadded up and spit out.

"Hellorrtherelittlelady," the big guy slurred, "and how are we tonight?" They'd parted at the stool to stand on either side of her and the fat one's head hung low to catch her eye. Weepy eye guy wiped his nose and looked eager. The smell of nacho-flavored alcohol made her want to gag so she focused on her hands, which were folded innocently in front of her.

"I think we need to get you another drink. Hey," Cowboy shouted over the din of the room, "how about some drinks down here."

Tom Jackson, Jackson's owner and master drink maker, was in the midst of story-telling. He stood like a conductor with his hands hanging high in the air and a ratty white dish towel dangling from one of them. The crowd was two deep with their mouths hanging open, listening to what surely were stories of the bar's beginnings. When Cowboy yelled, Tom's hands froze, then he slapped the bar with the towel making a loud crack before throwing it back over his shoulder where it came to rest like a dead animal at which time Tom continued with his story.

"Darn it," Gina muttered under her breath, then flapped with her elbows against the bellies pressed against her triceps.

"Hey, you! Bartender!" Cowboy hadn't noticed the suggestive move. "I'd like to get some beers down here."

"What is it with him?" he asked his buddy when Tom continued to ignore him.

"That's okay," Gina said. "I'm waiting for someone."

"Oh, come on, sweetheart, I bet you got a little bit of time for us. I been watchin' you all night and I don't think anyone's comin'. Hard to believe, if you asked me. Have a beer with us. We're harmless, ain't we, Everett?"

Everett smiled and wheezed and Gina thought if he wiped his nose one more time she was going to put a bend in his wind pipe.

Then Cowboy made a move that had probably worked at least once before. He lifted his heavy arm and draped it over her shoulders. Instantly, Gina caught hold of his thumb and twisted it hard, and with just enough torque to make him think she was going to take it off. The big guy squealed like a pig and lurched over the bar with his face pressed into the sticky wood.

"Well, I'm not," Gina whispered with her lips in his ear. Her voice was cold and hard. "I don't want to embarrass you but I think it would be best if you and Everclear over there went on back to your party." She released the thumb and it fell away like a piece of meat. Cowboy stumbled back, cussing as he held his thumb like a dead bird, then he and Everclear retreated.

The Coca-Cola clock over the door told her midnight had come and gone. She hated to admit it but Cowboy had been right about one thing. No one had noticed her.

She knew she looked good. The sheer blouse floated when she moved and the leather pencil skirt bound her legs so tightly she squeaked. She was also wearing enough jewelry to light the room. But for some strange reason, no one was biting.

It was 1998 and Gina knew she still looked younger than her thirty-three years. The skin around her mouth and eyes was soft and unlined and her hair was rich and dark, like the girl in the Breck commercial. Her body was toned like a body builder's but her hands were dainty with long, delicate fingers. Ballerina hands, her mother called them. But like the big guy said, no one was interested and she couldn't understand it, either. Tom's craggy voice, full of Texas twang and love of life, carried over the noise of the bar as he continued to make lazy swipes at the counter with the towel. She smiled a crooked smile. The quirky bartender was most of Jackson's charm.

"Fill 'er up?" Tom was suddenly in front of her and already pouring.

"Thanks." Gina said, then took a sip. She felt the burn as the soda slipped down her throat.

She'd been a regular at the neighborhood bar ever since she'd happened upon it three years ago while working a late night shift. The establishment sat squarely at the northeast corner of Maple Avenue and Wolf Street, in a part of Dallas that was difficult to describe. It was neither *Uptown*, the swanky niche of boutiques and restaurants for wealthy yuppies, nor was it downtown, that stuffy legoworld of high rises and hotels that appealed to the more serious condo dweller.

Tom hated change and over the years he'd done whatever he could to hide Jackson's among the tic tac toe of streets that kept outsiders wondering which way was north.

First, there was the wrought iron gate in the middle of a leaning fence that squeaked and hung off its hinges, then the Bourbon Street balcony and trees that stayed wrapped in Christmas lights all year long. From the street, one could barely see the front door. It was like he'd drawn a thick line in the sand to define his kingdom, and from there he sat and watched happily as the rest of the neighborhood transformed itself, not once but several times, into what Dallas in the 90's considered respectable and trendy. Jackson's, it was clear, would not be participating.

Gina studied the speckles of grey that marred the old glass mirror over the bar, then ran her fingers through her hair like a comb. The men were ignoring her, happy again at their table. She caught Tom's eye. The towel was quiet. Failure or no failure, it was time to call it a night.

CHAPTER 2

"Hello, Gina? Are you there? Hello?"

Earlier in the evening Gina had been standing in the bedroom closet of her downtown condo fighting with a tight red blouse when she heard the phone ringing. She hurried for it but the answering machine got it first.

"Hi, it's me, leave a message if you have to," her own voice said.

"Gina, hello, are you there?" her mother's voice began. "Are you going to pick up? Well, I'll just talk but pick up if you're there. I just realized while I was eating dinner that I hadn't talked to you about Louise Barrister's funeral tomorrow. You're going, aren't you? I think it's at eleven at the Presbyterian Church but I'd like to get there by ten-thirty. I'll be at Louise's house with Mona and Charlotte and oh I don't know who else from Garden Club but we'll have to get everything ready for the reception so why don't you come to the house about ten fifteen and we can ride together? I've got my handicapped sticker...Beep." The machine cut her off and Gina heard her eunuch-like cat Bad Guy drinking out of the toilet again. Both happened a lot.

The phone rang again. "Hello, Gina? Can you pick up? I wanted to tell you Garden Club is handling everything but we might need you girls to help in the kitchen after the funeral. We're expecting at least a hundred people. I'm pretty sure most of the other daughters will be there. Did I already say I could give you a ride?" There was only a second of a pause while her mother took a breath.

"Well, let me know in the morning. Or just be at the house by ten-fifteen and look for me. Louise's house looks so beautiful. You wouldn't believe how many flower arrangements people have sent over... Beep." The machine did it again.

When her mother mentioned the other daughters, Gina was fitting herself into a lacy black bra. She stopped, as a sour tendril of acid seeped into her stomach, the kind she used to get when her parents asked her to play the piano for company. The mixture of guilt and anger was her problem, but she knew it would stay with her until she could find something else to think about. Problem solved as she hooked the bra and started shuffling through her favorite shirts, determined to pick the most revealing one she could find.

When her mother said "we," she was referring to the Hillcrest Heights Garden Club, a Dallas institution of which her mother was a founding member. Of the thirty original members, twenty were alive and well. They were now in their seventies and eighties but they still held in their minds, or at least what was left of their minds, more than forty years' worth of gardening knowledge, family secrets, drama, and Robert's Rules of Order.

Gina truly loved them all. They were like second mothers to her and they were smart and sweet and gracious. But she also knew how dangerous they could be.

Once Garden Club got wind of anything that hinted at a wedding, baby, divorce, therapy, death, surgery, accident or wayward children, they latched on like mad turtles, arranging for 24-7 coverage or whatever else it took to get someone through the event. Whether it was an ordeal or celebration, the Club was like a geriatric SWAT team, mobilizing in minutes, day or night, whether one wanted them to or not. They brought food, arranged for services, manned the phones and/or delegated. Delegating, especially, was Gina's mother's gift.

Gina plunged a foot into a thigh-high black boot. Bad Guy had finished in the bathroom and languished across the pillow on her bed. He stretched out his front paws and shivered.

"I bet none of the other daughters are going out in a see-through shirt and leather boots," Gina said to Bad Guy as she pressed in her heel. "Oh no, they're all home in their perfect houses with yards, sitting in front of their TVs with their husbands and kids all snuggled up on the couch, having a nice quiet evening at home. But no, not me. I get asked to work and can't say no because I have nothing better to do."

Gina sucked in her stomach and worked the zipper up on the tiny piece of fabric meant to cover her rear end. She smoothed down the cheap leather. A heavy crystal necklace and matching earrings went on, then she planted herself in front of a mirror to analyze what she saw. Satisfied, Gina left for her favorite bar.

Just five more minutes, she thought, pushing the battered lime around in her glass before taking another sip. A new couple wandered through Jackson's front door and she watched them go to a dark corner booth. The man was tall with square shoulders and sandy brown hair that brushed his collar. He had a serious cowlick and kept brushing it back with large hands, then he leaned across the table toward the woman until their heads almost touched.

"May I join you?" Gina jumped, almost knocking over her drink. A man with a beer had tapped her on the shoulder then immediately taken a step back. He was either very shy or very experienced.

"Sorry, I didn't mean to scare you."

His face reminded her of a plush toy with lidless eyes. Gina rotated herself to give him a better view and watched as his eyes moved over her slowly. As expected, he liked what he saw and eased himself onto the stool next to hers.

"Robb," he said, extending a hand, adding, "with two Bs."

"Gina," she said without taking his hand. Her eyes, however, darted over his shoulder at Tom who was still at the other end of the bar. The bartender was staring back and the dish towel, the one that had been in his hand or over his shoulder for the last three hours, was gone.

Gina met Robb's hungry gaze. Her glossy red lips broke into a dazzling smile. "Nice to meet you, Robb with two Bs."

Robb almost choked on his spit. He coughed to clear his throat and his senses before asking, "Are you enjoying yourself?"

"No," she pouted. "I'm not at all."

He smiled too quickly and raised his beer to his lips, almost knocking out a tooth. Gina noticed the bottle was shaking. This one was going to be easy, she thought.

"That's too bad," he mumbled over the glass.

"I know, and I am so bored."

"I'll buy you another drink," he said, but Gina stopped him with a touch to his arm.

"No, thank you."

He eyed her.

"I was actually hoping for something a little bit stronger than a drink."

She could almost feel his desire as she played with the streaks of water on the wood left over from her drink.

"I assume you have some cash?" he asked, addressing the mirror

"Of course."

"Then maybe I can help. But it's outside, in my car." He watched her closely.

"I would really like that."

"Hey, have you ever been to Cancun? I just got back and you would not believe the water."

Gina pictured her ballerina hands around his neck. Tenderly, she reached over and touched his arm again. He immediately stopped talking.

"I'm sorry, Robb, but I'm very tired and I've been waiting all night long for someone just like you to come along. Would it be okay if we moved this along a little faster?"

Robb searched her eyes, then fumbled for his wallet and threw down a few dollars. She let him lift her off her stool, which he did easily. When she landed it was obvious she was six inches shorter and a hundred pounds lighter.

"Tight skirt," she said, pressing against his chest so that he could feel the heat of her body, then she pushed away and walked past him on her way toward the door.

Gina caught Tom's eye and waved a few fingers.

"Night, Tom," she called.

"Night, Gina, see you later."

"I guess you're a regular, here?" Robb asked as they emerged onto Jackson's front patio. It was late March and the red Christmas lights twinkled in the trees.

"Sort of."

The air smelled of rain as Gina slipped into the bucket seat of Robb's Camero. He hurried around to the driver's side and got in, then quickly hit the automatic locks before reaching under the front seat. He dangled several baggies under the dim dome light.

"They're so colorful," Gina said as she giggled.

"It's the newest thing. Flavored meth. What's your favorite flavor?"

"Hmmm, let's see," Gina mused, "blueberry?"

"That's my best seller."

Robb picked out a tiny baggie of a purplish powder and Gina handed him her money. As soon as he took the cash, she smoothly reached into her clutch and pulled out her badge.

"Sorry to have to tell you this, Robb, but I'd like to welcome you to Act 3. You are under arrest and I'm so glad because I really want to go home."

Robb's face drained into a tragic mask and she actually felt sorry for him which was probably why she didn't see it coming. He threw his elbow into her jaw then grabbed the driver's side door handle and slammed his body against the panel. The handle moved but the door didn't. Dazed, Gina tried grabbing his arm but the console was high and without climbing into his seat, there was no way she could get the leverage she needed. She flipped over and lunged with her back, pushing her full body weight on top of him and trapping him against his door with her legs locked against the opposite side.

Robb groaned with his face mashed against the glass. One arm was pinned down while his other arm flailed. She grabbed it and applied pressure at the wrist. He screamed in pain.

"That was a big mistake, Robb," Gina said, breathing hard. She tested her jaw to make sure nothing was broken, then pulled out the small gun she kept in her boot. Her jaw hurt so she gave an extra push against his body and squeezed at the pressure point on his wrist.

"Hey, I cahn breaff," he uttered helplessly.

"Good, now do you give up? I've got my gun pointed at your butt, by the way."

"I giff up, now geh off me."

Gina slowly unlocked her knees and lowered herself back into her seat, keeping the gun pointed at him. It was Robb's turn to feel over the half of his face that got the glass.

"I think you broke my cheekbone."

"I doubt it." Gina cursed the pencil skirt. She didn't have room for any cuffs and hadn't planned on needing them.

"Okay, Robb, time to go," she said, waving toward his door. "I want you to get out, very slowly, and put your hands on top of the car. Then we're going to walk over to my car and go downtown."

Like a guilty puppy, Robb unlocked the doors. He got out and stood as he'd been told, placing his hands flat on top of the car. Gina kept an eye on his torso and opened her door, then tried lifting her legs out of the car. But her left leg wouldn't lift. The heel was tangled in the weave of the carpet. With her eyes trained on Robb's belly, her heart began to race as she tried pulling at the boot. She wrenched it up and sideways in hopes of tearing it out of the threads but the fibers had purposely wrapped themselves around the stiletto and would not let go.

"Come on," she muttered, steeling a look into the blackness of the floorboard. When she looked up, she saw Robb's face in the driver's side window. At first, he looked curiously at her, but then his eyes travelled down her leg into the darkness that was the floorboard. Then they travelled back up. Their eyes locked, then he bolted into the night.

CHAPTER 3

Darn it, I forgot to cancel my hair appointment. Sweet Jesus, just let me get through this day. It was the morning of the funeral as Claire Sessions talked to her Lord like one would a constant companion. She was sure it also helped with her blood pressure. Feeling better, she put the pocket-sized calendar back into her purse and got out of the car.

Claire climbed the steps to the Barrister's kitchen door and let herself take a moment to catch her breath, fanning her chest with her dress for the breeze. It was not yet eight in the morning and the sun had already burned off any hope of coolness. Growing up in Texas she was used to the heat, but ever since she'd turned seventy, Claire was convinced it would be the humidity of these hot spring months that would kill her.

She'd gotten the call earlier in the week. She remembered it being much cooler then.

"Hello, Claire, this is Mona. I have some terrible, terrible news."

"What?"

"Louise Barrister is dead!"

As the Hillcrest Heights Garden Club's past and current president, Mona Johnson was used to getting to the point.

"She had a stroke while she was dividing her iris on Saturday. Can you believe it? I'm sure it was the humidity. The only reason I found out was because I ran into Dr. Wilcox at Dougherty's Pharmacy. They took her to Baylor and she passed away on Sunday. That's why she wasn't at church."

"Saturday? It's Monday. Why am I just now hearing about it? Why didn't anyone call me?"

"I am calling you, and I just found out myself and it's because Louise is, I mean *was*, Sunshine and Cloudy Weather so there wasn't anyone else to get the phone tree started. Claire, are you there?"

"I'm here, I'm just so stunned. And, oh no! She's going to miss our last flower show." Claire felt a twinge in her chest and wondered if she should take a pill.

"We can't think about that now," said Mona. "We've got things to do. Call your person on the phone tree and then call me right back." Mona hung up before Claire could say good-bye.

Claire found her list and called the next person, but then she decided not to call Mona back. She needed to make her lists. There were things to buy, assignments to be made, silver to polish. But before all that, Claire thought, her pen hovering over the paper, she needed to make a quick call to Frank.

"Howdy," the quivering voice answered.

"Hello, Frank? This is Claire, from Garden Club. Listen, honey, I'm so sorry to hear about Louise. How are you doing?" She listened for a moment while untwisting the phone cord, then jumped in because Frank couldn't seem to get to the point.

"Frank, I know this is such a sad time but you don't need to do a thing. Garden Club can make all those decisions. You know that's what we do best." She allowed Louise's husband to agree, then added respectfully, "Don't worry about a thing, someone will be right over. Now when are the boys getting in?"

Louise and Frank had two sons. Both had lost their minds and moved to Boulder, Colorado, right after college then married local women who would probably be thrilled to know Garden Club was handling all the details for their mother-in-law's funeral, not to mention the reception. Claire pondered that for a moment while Frank tried finding the piece of paper where he'd written down the details. She wondered if people even did funerals in Colorado anymore. They probably threw one's ashes off the nearest mountain.

Frank said something about plane flights then asked a question, a good sign that he wasn't completely lost.

"Yes, honey," Claire soothed, "we've discussed the graveside and we know exactly who to call. You can leave everything up to the Club. We loved Louise so much. She was like a second mother to us all."

Once Frank understood how things would go, Claire spent the rest of Monday, Tuesday, Wednesday and Thursday delegating. She was relieved when Friday finally came, as she stood outside the Barrister's kitchen door. Instinctively, she slapped a spot on her arm and when she pulled her hand away, there was a tiny smudge of blood and the beginning whelp of a mosquito bite. She looked down and saw the problem right away —a clay pot, knuckle-deep in brown water and larvae, sat inches from her foot. Claire grabbed hold of the railing, tucked a toe beneath the dish, and flipped it off the porch into the flower bed below.

"Ha," she said.

Garden Club had been birthed in the spring of 1955. Claire and her three best friends, Mona, SueBee, and Charlotte, had just graduated from Southern Methodist University. It was the same year *Life* had run a story on college women and named SMU a likely place to find a woman with charm, personality and beauty.

Within three months of graduation, the four friends were married and in their first homes. That next April, at bridge club, Mona, who by then had had a baby, announced that she was bored.

"Can't we find something to do that's more challenging than bridge?" she asked, trumping Charlotte's jack of clubs.

SueBee, who was pregnant with her first, lit up. "Let's start a garden club. My Aunt Louise is a Master Gardener, whatever that is. And she can make homemade rolls and rose-shaped butter pots."

Aunt Louise became the club's advisor and Mona named herself president. SueBee was in charge of horticulture, Charlotte was elected Social Chair, and Claire, secretary and treasurer. That first year they borrowed a constitution and by-laws from another club and decided on a limit of thirty members. Mona pulled the Club's name out of a hat, literally.

Claire smoothed a few frizzy grey hairs that had escaped from the tight bun at the base of her neck and propped open the screen door with her shoulder, then gave the kick plate a hard nudge with her sensible shoes.

She immediately smelled strong coffee. "Good morning, everyone. Why is it already so hot in here? Richard," a handsome black man with a shiny head unwrapping punch cups from a large box looked up, "do you mind going out to my car and bringing in some casseroles? I'm parked at the end of the circle drive."

"Yes, ma'am."

Claire felt a rush of cold air from a vent in the floor. She allowed herself a moment to stand still while the chill climbed up between her legs, then she hid her purse in the dryer and tied on an apron before surveying the room. Things appeared to be running smoothly. Two women from the catering company were already unpacking dishes while two more leaned into the center island making small piles of cut lemons and stuffed olives. All wore simple black shifts with starched white collars. Two or three men still looked cool in stiff cotton shirts buttoned up to the neck as they moved stacks of folding chairs out onto the back lawn.

Claire knew her three best friends, SueBee, Mona and Charlotte, would arrive soon and for the first hour, it would be the four of them making the most important decisions. Others of the club would come soon enough, then Claire would pair them off with the list of tasks she carried in her head.

Claire checked her watch. The funeral people would be coming by to pick up enough flower arrangements to decorate Louise's casket and the front of the church. Picking out which ones to take would be her responsibility, and in Claire's opinion, it was the most important task of all.

"The refrigerator is full of food and the icebox in the garage is already full too, Mrs. Sessions." Ruby, Richard's wife and Mona's housekeeper as long as she could remember, stood at the sink with both arms deep in the soapy water. "It's been nonstop."

"I guess we keep stacking things in the butler's pantry."

Richard returned with the casseroles and Claire set the timer on the double ovens then stepped aside as he slid them both in.

"Thank you, Richard. Come on, Ruby. Let's go check on the table." Ruby dried off her hands and followed Claire through the swinging door into the dining room where light from the chandelier bounced off a long mahogany table.

It was covered with the Club's silver collection of platters and bowls. An especially showy piece was the Grand Baroque tea service. It had an oversized tray, tea and coffee pots, sugar bowl, creamer, and a smaller urn for spoons. A large silver punch bowl sat at the other end of the table.

They'd begun the silver collection years ago, and added enough pieces over the years to handle any size function. In between parties, each piece stayed with whomever had won it at the last flower show. No one ever worried about who had what, and every piece always showed up when needed.

"It looks like we robbed a silver store, doesn't it, Ruby? Did you polish all these?"

"Last night," said the strong woman as she rubbed a prune-y finger to smooth a brush line. "The ladies dropped off everything they had and it all needed polishin'."

Claire frowned and looked more closely at the punch bowl.

"Wait a minute. That's not our bowl, is it?"

"I know. Miss Cynthia, she's the one that married Miss Louise's oldest boy, told me to use the Barrister's family bowl since it was already out. Do you want me to go get the Club's bowl? It's probably in the silver closet."

"No, no, that's alright," Claire said quickly. "Everything looks perfect." Claire shifted a Franciscan silver tray a quarter of an inch to the left. "I think the last time we had everything out was for that bridal shower for SueBee's son's new wife. If it weren't for weddings and funerals..."

"Ain't that the truth," Ruby said. "Speaking of weddings, how's your Gina?"

Claire sighed, "Who knows. I called last night and again this morning but just got the machine. All she does is work, work, work. I don't think she's had a date in months."

"She's on her own schedule. You don't have to worry about her."

"Of course I do," said Claire. "I was old when we had her and now she's taking so long to get married, I'm not going to get to see any grandchildren if she doesn't hurry up."

"She's still young."

"Thirty-three?"

"That's young, Miss Sessions. This is the nineties. People get married in their thirties and forties all the time. Now don't look like that!" She began rubbing on Claire's back. "Maybe you shouldn't think about it."

Back in the kitchen, Claire started on her secret recipe for sweet tea while Mona, who had just arrived with the others, went to work building a pyramid of finger sandwiches for an oversized silver tray with ornate handles. SueBee dusted lemon squares with powdered sugar and Charlotte was put in charge of taking calls.

"Do we need help with the flowers?" Charlotte relayed the question from the phone.

"Heavens no!" Claire called back. "We're a garden club for pity's sake."

Over the next hour, a slow and steady procession of respectable-looking women began to come through the kitchen door. All spoke to Ruby, dropped off purses in a downstairs guest bedroom, then reported to Claire for their assignments.

At ten, a van from the funeral home arrived to pick up the arrangements that Claire had selected and at approximately 10:30, the Garden Club got in line for the powder room before leaving for the church. Ginger, the youngest member of the club at sixty-six, was the only one asked to stay behind.

Hers was an important job. The family was told she would take care of answering the phone, plugging in the coffee and making sure the butter was set out just before noon. Also, Claire assured the family, Ginger could be counted on to make the house look occupied. Everyone knew bad people watched obituaries, and even though there was a party staff of six going about their business and the family had purposefully not included the location of the reception in the paper, the Club always left someone behind to give the family peace of mind.

Claire also needed Ginger to keep an eye on Louise's silver closet while they were gone. Right after Ruby's comment about the punch bowl, she had casually made her way back to the special room that kept out moisture and light for the Barrister's large collection of silver. When the door closed behind her, she pulled on a string to light the room. There, beneath the bottom shelf, were six plump grocery sacks of marijuana, neatly labeled and ready for delivery.

CHAPTER 4

The first thing Gina remembered when she woke up Friday morning was the look on Robb's face when he realized he was the luckiest guy in the world. With a ferocious growl, she'd ripped her heel from the floorboard and jumped out of the car to give chase. But by that time, plush toy Robb was long gone. Still, it didn't take long to find him, and then there was the booking and writing up the report. It was after three before she got to go home to a very hungry and angry cat. Bad Guy didn't like it when she kept him waiting.

Gina got dressed. She'd decided to wear pants for this assignment, and picked up a coffee at the 7-Eleven outside her building. By ten she was leaning against a two-story warehouse at the corner of Malcolm X and Main in a struggling neighborhood just across the highway that bordered downtown Dallas. For decades it had been a picture of poverty, with beaten down warehouses made of crumbling brick and dingy storefronts that mostly attracted the homeless. But over the past few years, people with enough patience had seen something worth fighting for. One by one, the old buildings were being converted to better uses.

A construction crew was hard at work in front of her. Gina watched as a bathtub-sized shovel went in and out of a deep hole in the middle of the street about twenty yards away. In between bites, the shovel was allowed to rest on the concrete surface and when it did, she felt the sidewalk vibrate. A withered-looking figure stood in the middle of the street with a yellow flag to slow down the occasional car but mainly he watched Gina. His face was like a piece of wet leather and his shoulders so non-existent that the orange safety vest he wore kept falling off.

The shovel slammed against the pavement. Gina winced and shifted her weight from one foot to the other. The high heels made her feel like she was standing on her tiptoes, which made it hard to concentrate on the warehouses across the street.

A few stragglers walked by her on their way to jobs on the other side of the highway. They gave her a disapproving look before entering a coffee shop just a few doors down. Gina checked her watch again, then looked east into the sun at a wall of office buildings that rose like headstones over the freeway.

A movement across the street caught her eye. A man appeared out of nowhere as he made his way along the side of the warehouse toward her. Confused, Gina's eyes searched the wall of the warehouse until she made out the faint outline of a doorway.

"So that's where you've been hiding," she said, shifting her weight again and stretching a relieved foot.

The wall was a neighborhood icon. Kids from a nearby art school had painted a gigantic mural of a mystical purple dragon escaping from his dungeon to attack the people of earth. His mouth was open in an angry roar and there were flames coming out in waves of fiery purples and greens. Millions of tiny specks of white represented his victims and covered the lower third of the painting. Everyone knew the 'Dragon Wall' but never before had she realized that the monster's black mouth was actually a door. No wonder he'd stayed hidden.

Gina stepped out of the shadow toward the bus stop just a few feet away. As the man drew closer, obviously headed for the coffee shop, Gina caught his eye and smiled, recognizing the suspected drug dealer's face from his photos. Her heart beat faster in her chest and she felt the weight of her gun in the curve of her back. She held on to the pole as she smoothed her black leather pants into her boots, then raised up just as the man arrived.

"Excuse me, can you spare a cigarette?"

The man slowed and stopped, then pulled out a pack.

"You're working kinda' early, aren't you?"

"I'm just waiting for a bus," she said.

"Sure you are." He got out a cigarette for both of them. "I'm going to get some coffee next door. Would you like to join me?"

"Thanks, but I've got someplace to go. I'm probably going to be late, too."

"Really?"

"Yeah, my mother wants me to come to this family thing."

"Okay, if you say so. But if you change your mind, I'll be in there," he pointed with his cigarette.

"Thanks." She watched him disappear inside the coffee bar, then quickly took out a baggie and put the cigarette he'd given her inside the plastic. She hurried across the street in her tall boots, waved at the guy in orange, and walked quickly along the graffiti wall to the hidden door. Gina pulled out a miniscule camera and took several snapshots of the door, the wall, and any cars that were parked on the street. Finding out where he lived was the first piece of the puzzle and later this afternoon, she'd get these pictures to the guys. But right now, Gina had to get away for at least an hour. She had a funeral to go to.

It was difficult walking in her heels. At five feet, five inches, she had long legs and a quick stride but had to concentrate on the sidewalk's deep cracks. At the same time, her mind was racing. *I'm going to be late,* she thought, *that's not good.* A heel caught in one of the cracks and she winced in pain before righting herself and hurrying on. She would probably kill herself trying.

Gina had been taught from an early age that being on time was just as important as writing thank you notes the same day of the party and serving from the left and clearing from the right. But those were the easy ones, Gina thought.

Rule Number One. "It's very important," Gina's mother repeated and most often in the company of strangers, "if you're paying for something, then make sure you get what you paid for." In other words, *Stand up for yourself. If you don't, no one else will.*

Rule Number Two. This was shared most often in a club member's kitchen while filling the Garden Club's silver trays with finger sandwiches for a wedding shower or flower show. There were several versions but the one she knew best was, "And don't you come in the front door, honey. Use the kitchen door." This meant that she, and anyone else helping to make things run smoothly and gracefully, was family.

Gina remembered the exact moment her mother had shared with her Rule Number Three. It was when she was thirteen and her father had recently left them. She was walking through the house with a basket full of dirty laundry when she suddenly stopped and with a stern look on her face said, "No matter what happens, Gina, if you ever get in trouble with the law, or get pregnant, or get fat, whatever, you can always come home."

Gina remembered rolling her eyes. What had her mother expected? She'd only been thirteen.

Trying not to break any laws, she raced across town to the Presbyterian church. It was in the Hillcrest Heights neighborhood where most of the garden club members lived and now their daughters and their families lived there, too. Her mother was the only club member who lived outside the Heights in a tiny house not too far away. Gina suddenly jerked the wheel and made a sharp turn into the parking lot making the tires of the Jeep squeal. Before getting out, Gina put on the pink lipstick she carried for such occasions.

Gina opened the heavily carved doors with their stained glass windows. The sound of the organ hit her and she could see the people already taking their seats in the front three rows that had been reserved for family only. The Barristers were obviously a big family. She quickly took a seat in the back row and noticed a few of the other daughters looking her way. They all smiled, genuinely, and no seemed to even notice she was late.

Sunlight poured through the windows of the half-full sanctuary, reflecting off the heads of the crowd. Down front, the shiny pipes of the organ stretched toward Heaven and then Gina spotted the ladies of Garden Club sitting in the row directly behind the family. That's where they always sat. From there they could easily pet a relative.

Mona Johnson was sitting on the aisle. Her back was militarily erect and she wore a glamorous black hat with lacy netting pulled down over her face. Next to her was Cleeve, her husband. Gina liked Cleeve. He was a real charmer who had only gotten better looking with age. Next to him was Charlotte, the kindest lady anyone could meet, Gina thought. Taller than the rest, she looked regal even from behind. Sitting next to Charlotte was SueBee who looked like a miniature doll with a floral sweater draped softly across her shoulders. According to a message Gina's mother had left her several days ago, SueBee's husband was still recovering from hip replacement surgery. Finally, on the end of the row and closest to the exit, was Gina's mother, Claire.

The minister asked the audience to bow their heads and began reciting the Lord's Prayer. Gina didn't, but continued to stare at her mother's head. Slowly, her mother's head rose, and then turned, her eyes sweeping back and forth over the bowed heads of the small audience. Eventually, she spotted Gina and they both smiled, then Claire turned back around and her shoulders relaxed.

Gina sighed. From a distance, they were always fine.

"What have I done to so completely send you into this other orbit, Gina?" her mother had argued less than a week ago. "I don't understand why you'd want your life to revolve around that police station. And now you want to be a senior detective? What kind of life is that? With your brains and looks and upbringing, why would you want to be a policeman, or police person, or whatever it is I'm supposed to call you. I was over at SueBee's last week when Helen stopped by with the children and she talked about her volunteer work with the symphony. I wish you had time to do some of those things. I asked her to give you a call."

"I wish you hadn't. I'll call her in a few years, but not now.

"I don't think you get out enough with young people your own age. I think Charlotte's daughter goes on an annual girls' trip and…"

"Mom, please, stop with the other daughters. They're a lousy frame of reference. I'm fine, Mom. I'm happy. Really. "

Her mother looked unconvinced. She turned away, but not before making a visual sweep of the condo. Gina's cat Bad Guy was splayed across the back of the couch but Claire's attention lingered on the bookcases, cluttered and disorganized, then quickly came back to her daughter. It was as if she hadn't heard anything Gina had said.

" They're such nice girls, Gina."

"Of course they are. But I have a different life. Honestly, we have nothing in common."

'That isn't quite true," Gina had almost said. The daughters actually shared one very important thing and that was that none of them wanted to be in a garden club.

"Amen," the minister said, as the organ bellowed "Amazing Grace." Gina noticed the mothers' row immediately began inching their way across their pew so they could be the first ones out the side exit. Inching was typical Garden Club behavior, but today they seemed to be in more of a hurry than usual.

CHAPTER 5

"What in the world are we going to do about the sacks in the silver closet?" Claire asked Charlotte as she unlocked the door of her Chrysler. By the time she got behind the wheel, her friend had already put on her seat belt and was gripping the door handle.

"For pity's sake, Charlotte, we haven't even left the parking lot. Wave at that car over there. See if he'll let me butt in." Charlotte's hand fluttered and the other car stopped to let them pass.

"Those sacks are the least of my worries. What about all the plastic stuff? Louise had so much and I don't know how long it's going to take us to pull it apart. And then what do we do with it?"

Claire sped up to get through a yellow light and took the next right turn. "We'll have to talk to Mona and SueBee. I just hope no one gets in there before we get the sacks out."

"Do you think we could sell the equipment?" Charlotte asked. "Maybe Jonas would want to buy it? Or we could just give it to him."

"Jonas? No, I don't think so," said Claire. Jonas was Mona's nephew and had been their delivery boy ever since he'd turned sixteen. "He's from the other side of the family. Very sweet but not that smart. I think we should let him stick to deliveries."

"It's a lot of stuff," said Charlotte, "and my closet's full. I still can't believe we went the whole week and no one thought to look. It would have been so much easier to get it out before the family got here." Charlotte flinched as Claire whipped around a car in the slow lane, then thought of something else. "We need to keep a close eye on the daughters, especially Gina since she's a cop."

Claire responded by speeding up and then slid into the turn lane, made a sharp right, then halfway down the block and hardly slowing down she whipped left into Louise's driveway, stopping inches away from the garage door. Charlotte's head was tucked tightly into her chest, her hands clutching the seatbelt strap beneath her chin.

"We're here!"

"If you say so," said Charlotte, her eyes clenched shut.

The rest of the Club, those who'd been assigned to kitchen duty, arrived and began transferring food from the kitchen to the table. The smell of garlic and cheese filled the dining room as they put out the tetrazini and cheese grits. Claire pulled Ginger aside for a few words in private, then sent her to the store for ice before lighting the sterno under the casseroles.

To calm her nerves, Claire checked on the silver closet. Nothing had been disturbed. Out in the hallway, she found an old iron doorstop and pushed it against the door, hoping it would make it clear that the silver closet was off limits.

"Whatcha doin', Claire?" Cleeve, Mona's husband, had suddenly appeared behind her.

"Just finishing up. What are you doing? Where's your wife?"

"Outside. I never expect to see her at these things. I just wander around by myself looking for male companionship."

"You poor thing," said Claire, taking his arm and leading him back toward the dining room, "may I put you to work? Would you please check on the family at the front door? Make sure they don't need anything? If they're hungry or need a glass of water? A chair?"

Cleeve seemed grateful for the mission and headed off in the direction of the front door.

At the table, Claire noticed Charlotte's daughter Brooke admiring the food. Like her mother, she was perfectly dressed, and SueBee's daughter, Helen, who usually looked frazzled, stood beside her in a lovely tea dress. Claire decided the kitchen could survive without her for a few more minutes.

"Brooke, Helen," she said, pecking both on the cheek, "I'm so glad you were able to come. Are the children here?"

"Just Angela," said Brooke. "I decided to let her miss school. She's the only one who's really old enough to remember Louise. I've already sent her to the kitchen to help."

"Thank goodness mine are all in school," offered Helen.

Helen looked so much like SueBee, Claire thought. Both were beautiful without makeup and from watching Helen handle her three kids like a ringmaster, she could only imagine what SueBee must have been like.

"I'm so glad you're here," said Claire. "Get a plate and go outside. And don't miss the dessert table. And if you see dirty dishes starting to pile up, feel free to bring them to the kitchen. Helen, your mother's already out there waiting for you."

"We will, but I think we're going to do a quick tour of the house first. Mother said it might be our last chance," and they started for the living room.

"Wait!" Claire shouted, lunging for Helen's arm, "have you gone through the receiving line?" Their expression told her they had not. "Heavens, girls, you have to do that first," she said, herding them toward the front door.

"That's okay, we're going to sign the book later," said Brooke. "The line's all the way out the door and down the sidewalk."

"Oh but no, no, no, no," Claire answered. "That's not the way you've been raised. No excuses. You must go through the line. Coming in the kitchen door because you're like family is one thing but everyone else, well, it's just good manners to give your condolences face to face. Louise would want that. Don't worry, there will be plenty of food when you're done. Then come straight outside and sit with us." Reluctantly, the girls let themselves be guided, until something on the dining table caught Brooke's eye.

"How gorgeous," she murmured softly, reaching out to touch the raised motif of an enormous silver punch bowl in the center of the table. The arrangement inside included at least a dozen white camellias and even with all the food smells, Claire caught a whiff of a slightly sweet perfume.

"Is this the Club's bowl?" Brooke asked reverently.

"Of course. Both your mothers' names are on there somewhere, now keep walking."

"Do you think I could borrow it?" asked Brooke. "I'm giving a par..."

"Nope," Claire interrupted, "now go get in line or the food will all be gone. Come outside when you're done." Reluctantly, the girls moved off through the crowd. Claire looked for any sign of Gina, then raised her eyes to Heaven.

Back in the kitchen, Ruby was up to her elbows in dirty dishes.

"Go outside, Miss Sessions, get off your feet. We've got it under control in here."

Claire counted at least six club members in the already crowded kitchen. "I guess you're right, Ruby. I'll be outside if you need me."

She walked across the large stone patio that overlooked the back lawn. Large pots planted with tall fronds and trailing ivy decorated the low wall that separated the patio from the yard. Family and friends sat or stood in small groups at the round tables whose long white tablecloths fluttered in the early afternoon breeze.

The grass sloped gently downward toward a swimming pool and just beyond was a perfect line of cherry laurels that created a natural boundary for the property. A walkway of crushed pink granite wound like a stream among the two dozen tables, each one set with folding chairs that had also been draped in white. She soon spotted her friends, and went to join them.

Claire took a seat between Grace, also a member of Garden Club, and SueBee. Mona lowered her sunglasses, revealing marble-sized eyes. Claire wondered, as she often did, why anyone would hide the cheekbones of Mount Rushmore behind plastic, even if they did cost eight hundred dollars. It was something she would never understand.

"Hello, ladies," Claire said.

"I'm glad you finally got out of that kitchen," said Mona. She waved down a waitress who was carrying a tray of cups and a silver coffee urn. "What would you like to drink?

Grace's eyes darted conspicuously over her own cup and saucer.

"Grace?" SueBee spoke to her in a calming tone. "It's decaffeinated. Is that what you're worried about? It's not too hot, is it? Would you like sugar and cream?"

Grace took a quick breath and tried to smile. "Yes, thank you. Sugar?"

SueBee stirred in a spoonful. Everyone waited but Grace didn't taste it.

"How's she doing?" Claire whispered to Mona.

"Been like this the whole time."

Grace's hands remained in her lap while her eyes darted nervously from cup to table to friends. She wasn't much older than the others. Mona and SueBee were almost sixty-eight and Claire had just turned seventy-two even though everyone thought she was seventy. Still, Grace looked much older. Her skin sagged around her mouth and her hair was a drab grey. Claire made a mental note to call the aide who visited once a day and insist they do something with her hair.

Claire accepted a cup of tea, then got quickly to the point. "We've got a few minutes because I sent Brooke and Helen to the receiving line, but they'll be out here soon. I have no idea when Gina's coming, or Sheralyn." She looked at Mona. "What in the world are we going to do about Louise's silver closet? I still can't believe none of us thought about it all week."

"I could probably get all the sacks in my trunk," said SueBee.

"We need at least two cars," said Mona. "But I hate putting it in my Mercedes. Cleeve might smell it."

"I'm not worried about that," said SueBee. "My car already smells like fertilizer."

Brooke's fifteen-year-old suddenly appeared and put two pieces of Italian Cream cake in front of SueBee and Grace.

"Thank you, Angela," SueBee said. "Did your mother put you to work?"

"Of course she did," Angela said, angling her head at the house. "Grandmother's up there, too."

"Well then tell your grandmother we all said you are doing a bang up job, and thank you for my cake." SueBee tested the cake with her fork. "You know, I think this is my recipe. Do you want a bite? Mona? Claire?" Mona shook her head no and waited for Charlotte's granddaughter to move a safe distance away.

"Back to our problem," said Mona. "You can't get all that equipment in the trunk of your car, SueBee. I guess I'll have to use the Mercedes. Maybe if we use plastic garbage bags, but then there's all that equipment. I still can't believe it. Louise was always so prepared. I hope she didn't say anything about it in her will."

Claire leaned in. SueBee and Mona did the same.

"When do we do it? The family's going to be here at least two more days."

Grace chuckled, her hands clasped in her lap while her eyes darted to the other tables.

"What's so funny, Grace?" Mona asked.

"I don't know."

"Do you know what we're talking about?"

"No, I don't think so."

"Eat your cake, Grace," said SueBee, "it's very good."

"Really, SueBee, she'll eat her cake if she wants to. We're not going to feed it to her," insisted Mona.

" I saw Sheralyn come through the kitchen," said SueBee.

"Surprise, surprise. She's here to see the house."

Charlotte sat down hard in a chair.

"Nice of you to join us, Charlotte. We're trying to make a decision here," said Mona.

Charlotte ignored her. "Who-wee, my dogs are barking. Hello, darlings." She threw kisses all around and gave Grace a special touch. "Mona, honey, I just left Sheralyn in the foyer. She looked like a million bucks and I think, I really do, that she was studying those flower arrangements."

"Oh, please. She came to see the house. She wants to see all of Louise's things so she can go home and copy them. That's what she does."

"That's sort of what I do, or at least *did* when I was her age," said SueBee. "You're too hard on her, Mona."

"I agree," said Charlotte. "She's a dear. And oh, by the way, SueBee, I saw Helen. She's not pregnant is she?"

"Bite your tongue." SueBee leaned toward Charlotte. "We're tawkin about how to shut down Louise's gahden." Her Southern roots showed up more when she whispered.

"What garden? The irises?"

"Oh, for pity's sake, Charlotte," huffed Mona.

"The *other* garden," whispered Claire.

"May I make a suggestion?" said SueBee, her delicate hands wrapped around a cup. It was a rhetorical question, of course. Everyone listened to SueBee. She'd had four children in five years, all while staying active on three non-profit boards, and currently corralled thirteen grandchildren.

"First," she began, looking at Claire, "we wait for Gina to leave. Once she's out of the picture, we each grab a couple of sacks and put them in our cars. We carry them out like we are taking out our dishes. When everyone's gone and the family's upstairs, Mona and I will find some of those extra-large trash bags and haul everything straight into our cars. If anyone sees us, we'll tell them we're taking the Club's silver over to Mona's for next week's flower show. That's mostly true. Charlotte, you and Claire need to stand guard."

Claire looked over SueBee's shoulder toward the house. "That receiving line must have been really long."

"I still can't believe we're about to have our last flower show," Charlotte said. "At least we have the business. That should keep our brain cells in good shape."

The others agreed.

"We've been at this a long time," said Claire, almost to herself. "Since '89, or was it '88?"

"Eight-nine," said SueBee.

"You and Louise started us, isn't that, right?" asked Claire.

"I think it was 1990," said Mona.

"No, it was eighty-nine," said SueBee. "I remember because Helen had just had the twins, and then Lucille Ball died and I was turning sixty and feeling so old. That's when Louise found those squished up cigarettes in her son's jacket."

Mona smiled faintly. "She called me first."

Charlotte continued. "And then you called me. I don't think Louise even knew how to work a lighter."

"I'd had teenagers so I knew exactly what those things were," said Mona. "Louise called me first, and then you, and told us about an old friend who was so sick and the family was having fits because the nurse they had coming out to the house wasn't doing squat to help with the pain. Louise couldn't stand it one more minute, not being able to do anything, and then she found those cigarettes. She felt like it was a sign from God."

"I don't think Gina ever did drugs," reflected Claire.

"You were lucky," said Charlotte. "Gina was always a good girl."

Mona continued. "Louise's friend took one puff and suddenly he felt so much better. It was such a relief to everyone. After that, well…"

"The rest is history," said Claire.

"Louise was getting old herself. She had a lot of friends moving into those retirement homes and most of them felt like they were looking down the barrel of a shotgun. So, thanks to Madam President," Charlotte nodded to Mona, "we decided, 'Hey, we're a garden club. Let's do some good and learn to grow it ourselves. So we did."

"We have become quite the experts," Mona finished, sucking in her cheeks, pretending to take a drag.

"Please, Mona, stop that," said Claire, looking toward the house. "Gina will be here any minute."

CHAPTER 6

After the service, it took Gina ten minutes to get out of the church parking lot. By the time she got to the Barrister's home, a line of cars beginning at the valet stand snaked down the street, so she swung her Jeep up a side street and took the first open spot. Gina checked herself in the mirror and hurriedly put on more lipstick. She was still wearing the boots and tight pants.

It was a beautiful day. The lawns were ten shades of green and the fifty-year-old trees were like tall buildings, their branches heavy with another ten shades. Somehow the sun managed to appear in circles of light that danced around her and made the atmosphere glow over the sidewalk as she side-stepped a million greenish-blue pods that had fallen from a Bald Cypress. The pods were her mother's favorite color.

The Barrister home was a Georgian two-story brick with four strong pillars and an upstairs balcony, giving it a *Gone With The Wind* presence. As Gina got closer, the introductions began.

"Now whose daughter are you?" The question came from a blond woman, close to her age, dressed in a fitted black dress and pearls. Her husband trailed behind her with a tray of cookies. Gina looked down at her leather pants from the morning and suddenly felt like they had shrunk two sizes. The place at the back of her neck started to sweat.

"I'm Claire's daughter," she answered, pretending to study the house.

"Oh, that's right. You've probably forgotten, I'm Mary Louise, SueBee's second son's second wife. We aren't around much 'cause we moved back to Atlanta. That's where I'm from. SueBee thought we should come, since my husband grew up with the Barrister boys. Says they used to raise hell at those picnics the mothers had out at Mona's ranch."

Gina had never seen the round pink face.

"Who is that over there?" Gina asked, pointing to an older couple.

"Oh, that's not a mother. She was the boys' Sunday School teacher, years ago. It looks like the whole church is going to be here today. Anyway, she's got to be a hundred. You think?"

Just then, another pretty blonde sidled up between Gina and Mary Louise. "You're Claire's daughter, aren't you?"

Gina nodded. When another thirty-something blonde got close enough to ask Mary Louise the 'whose daughter are you' question, Gina veered right toward the driveway.

"Gina!" The kitchen's screen door had barely slammed closed behind her when Ruby saw her. Thick black arms emerged from the sink and she held them, dripping, toward Gina.

"Hi, Ruby," she said, her voice muffled until Ruby let go, then they hugged quickly again, laughing as they did. Ruby pushed Gina away and looked hard into her face, then her eyes traveled up and down her body. The smile faded.

"Girl, what are you doing coming in through the kitchen and dressed like that? You know you shouldn't be wearing pants to Miss Louise's going away party. And don't think you're fooling me with that pink lipstick."

"I'm wearing black."

Ruby's eyes opened wide as she leaned back to get a good look at the whole picture.

"Have you ever thought about trying to make a good impression? You look like one of those nasty girls. Somebody needs to sit you down and make you have a serious discussion about what it takes to take care of what the Lord God has given you. And from the looks of you..."

She stopped and looked harder.

"Are you tired or sick? Cause you have circles under your eyes." She reached out a finger. "Is that a bruise on your chin?"

"I had to work," said Gina, touching her chin tenderly, "but for Pete's sake, Ruby, these are my work clothes, I've told you that. I didn't have time to change." Ruby noticed a tattoo on the inside of Gina's wrist. "It's fake."

"Tell that to your mother. She's worried about you."

Gina picked up a strawberry from a Tupperware bowl and said, "I know. That's why I'm staying close to you," before popping the fruit in her mouth.

"I don't know how long I'm going to be able to tell her not to worry with a straight face. It would make her so happy if you'd get married. I don't think you're even trying." Ruby suddenly froze and looked Gina in the eye. "Are you a lesbian?"

"No!"

"I'm just askin'. So what was your mother sayin' about you being up for some sort of a promotion?"

Gina rolled her eyes. "Does the whole world know about that? Yes, I've applied for a promotion but a lot depends on some test results. I've worked undercover for five years and I think I've earned it."

Ruby turned back to the sink. "Too bad your mother doesn't think you can meet a nice man at a police station."

"At least she doesn't think I'm gay."

"Uh huh. Well, get in there," Ruby said. "The family's at the door."

"No, thank you. I've spent whole receptions in receiving lines."

Gina hid behind the swinging door into the dining room and looked through the crack to study the table, then stuck her nose in the space and smelled her mother's chicken tetrazzini. She pictured whole pieces of tender white meat smothered in a creamy sauce of fresh garlic, butter, salt and pepper. There would also be tiny pieces of sautéed mushrooms and a hint of paprika to give it a bite. Her mouth began to water.

"Where is Mother, by the way?" she asked Ruby. "Is she around?"

"She better be outside and off her feet with the rest of the Musketeers. They've been here all week, morning to night. I'd be exhausted if I were them but those old ladies just keep on going. It's like they get a dose of something every day. Must be the act of service that energizes them." Ruby shook her head at the dishwater. "I don't know how they do it."

"Good. I'm going to get something to eat."

Gina ignored the stares as she walked slowly around the dining room table. Her eyes darted from silver tray to silver bowl, trying to decide whether something should go on her plate or directly into her mouth. She took a large spoonful of the tetrazzini then picked off a large brownie from a silver tray. Underneath the brownie, the tray was etched with writing. They were the names of the ladies of garden club, and right beneath the brownie was her mother's name.

Out of the corner of her eye, Gina saw Brooke and Helen shaking Frank's hand in the receiving line. She quickly put a few more things on her plate, then turned back toward the kitchen but ran into Sheralyn, who was coming out of the kitchen carrying a silver Revere bowl of strawberries.

"Oh, sorry!" Sheralyn said, setting the bowl on the table. "Gina! How are you?"

By then, Brooke and Helen had entered the dining room. "Finally," said Brooke, "we've been in that receiving line forever."

"Yummy," said Helen, picking up a plate and loading it with cheddar balls, strawberries and stuffed mushrooms. "I'm starving."

Sheralyn was married to Mona's son Bryan. His first wife had run off with the church's choir director. She was beautiful, a twenty-something beauty queen from Arkansas.

"You look gorgeous, Sheralyn," Brooke said, before turning to Gina. It was unavoidable. Beginning with the icicle earrings, her eyes then travelled over the black leather pants, then stalled at the stiletto-heeled boots.

"I came from work," Gina blurted out.

"Of course you did. Don't worry about it, who cares?" said Brooke. "You look cool."

"Sure," said Gina. She looked longingly toward the kitchen then at the other daughters and saw they were wearing hose.

"Oh no, you don't," Brooke said, reading her mind. "The moms are waiting for us outside."

"I shouldn't go out there," Gina said, pulling away. "I think I should stay in the kitchen."

"Why?" Brooke said. "You came from work, right?"

"I think what you do is so interesting," said Sheralyn. "Let's all get a plate and go outside. They're waiting."

Gina followed the other three daughters out the back door. Standing on the patio, they surveyed the lawn until they spotted their mothers at a faraway table.

Brooke sidled up alongside Gina. "Anyone want to bet how long it takes before they ask us to start our own club?"

"Ten minutes," guessed Sheralyn.

"I'm betting five," said Helen.

"If that," said Gina, digging deep for courage before edging around the others and heading across the lawn.

CHAPTER 7

"Oh goodness, here they come," said Claire, swiping the pretend cigarette from Mona's lips. "Oh no, look what Gina's wearing. What am I going to do with her?"

The reception was in full swing and since the second shift had taken over, Claire and the others watched as their daughters floated back and forth between the tables on their way to join them. There were large swaths of shade against the grass and the guests had dragged the tables to find them. The temperature had slowly risen, so large fans which had been ordered in advance were being set up on along the out skirts. The grass was an irresistible green carpet to the children dressed in party clothes who were now chasing each other with colorful pinwheels.

Brooke sat next to her mother.

"Hello, Grace, how are you?" Grace nodded but continued to stare at her cake.

Helen pulled up a chair next to SueBee while Sheralyn took the last empty seat next to her mother-in-law.

"Isn't this a gorgeous house?" said Sheralyn.

Mona's eyebrows arched above her dark glasses. Gina found an extra chair from the next table and placed it behind Claire.

"There's room at the table, Gina, we can all move back."

"That's okay, Mom. I'm fine."

"Wasn't that a beautiful service?" said Brooke. "Louise would have loved it and the flowers were amazing." Everyone nodded in agreement.

"So how did you all escape from the kitchen?" asked Helen.

"We did our shift this morning," said SueBee.

"The table looks so pretty," Helen said. "That silver..." her voice trailed off.

Charlotte took a deep breath and reached for the hands of the daughters on either side of her. She looked deeply into their eyes.

"Why won't you girls start your own garden club?"

"I win," said Helen.

"Mother," Brook warned, taking back her hand.

"Time is running out," Charlotte pleaded. "Look around, we're dying. What's to become of all our traditions?"

"Mother, please."

"This is the perfect example of why you need to start a club," Charlotte said. "Who is going to help with *your* funeral? Because I certainly don't plan on being available."

"I think we'll be fine," Brooke answered.

"No, you won't. You need someone to answer the door and the phone and tell the caterer to use the kitchen door, and count the spoons afterward, and someone always needs to bring you a glass of water while you're in the receiving line, not to mention who's going to tell people if you need more sweet or salty on the table." She stopped to take a breath. "Helen, honey, don't you see?"

Helen smiled, shaking her head.

"I think that's what the caterer is for," said Gina from behind.

Claire turned in her chair and almost immediately Gina leaned forward and whispered, "I came straight from work."

Claire could only turn back around, but not before whispering back, "That is not a good pink for you."

"The caterer, exactly," Brooke said, giving Gina a thumbs up.

"Chester Crown!" Grace shouted. "That's his name. I've been trying to remember all day. Whatever happened to that boy, Chester Crown?" The eruption was enough to startle everyone.

"Oh, he's dead, honey, long time," Mona said, recovering first.

"He is?" Grace said, looking very disappointed.

Mona turned to Charlotte. "For pity's sake, stop begging them, Charlotte. Like intelligence, the love of gardening has skipped a generation. We'll just have to set our sights on the next one. Next week will be our last flower show and that's that."

"So it's true?" asked Brooke. "The Club is really calling it quits?"

"Bite your tongue, Brooke. We do not quit," said Mona.

"Because it's not allowed," said Gina. "Mom told me. No one is allowed to quit, isn't that right, Mom?"

"I believe I said we keep things simple," explained Claire to the other daughters.

"Right," said Gina. "So no attendance requirements but if you miss a meeting you get saddled with a job."

Claire interrupted. "That is true. I was absent one time so they fined me a dollar *and* I found out I'd been volunteered to buy the president's turnover gift."

"And you can move away or die, but never quit."

SueBee interrupted Gina. "We're not quitting. We've just decided to slow down. Next week will be our last flower show. That's all."

Claire turned around. "Are you sick? Your eyes look like you're getting sick."

"I'm just tired, I had to work late."

"Would you please move your chair up to the table so I don't have to keep doing these gymnastics?"

There was an awkward silence while Gina moved her chair in line with the others.

"How are the boys?" Claire directed her question to Sheralyn.

"Wonderful, but you know boys. They keep me busy, eating me out of house and home." She was beaming. "I'm just so thankful I get to stay home with them."

Brooke and Helen made agreeing comments.

"This is so interesting," said Gina under her breath. Claire was tempted to pinch her leg.

"Soooo," Brooke finally began, "if there aren't going to be any more flower shows, what about the Club's silver collection? Would you like us to help you store it?"

"No, thank you, but nice try," Mona said.

"If you had your own garden club…" Charlotte began.

"Melinda! Melinda Rawlins!" Grace suddenly came to life.

"Oh, Grace, she's dead, too," Mona quickly answered.

"Is she really? Dead, too?" Grace was crushed. "I can't believe it, they're all dead."

"Mom," Gina whispered, "do you need me to help you take stuff home? I can be a little late getting back to work."

"Heavens no," Claire said sharply. "I'm fine. No need."

"I can get the heavy stuff."

"I'm not an invalid, Gina." Her eyes dropped to her daughter's wrist where she saw the tattoo. "And I know you need to get back to work."

"I can stay until you need to pack up," Brooke volunteered to Charlotte.

"Oh no, honey, we're all fine. Really."

"Mom? Do you...?" Helen started.

"Helen, we're all fine," repeated Claire. "We know you girls have plenty to do, as do we." Claire winked at the others.

Again the table went silent.

"Have you heard anything about your test, Gina?" Charlotte asked.

Gina glared at her mother.

"She won't hear anything for a few more days, so we're not talking about it."

"I hope we'll see everyone next Saturday at the flower show," said Mona.

"Of course," they all agreed.

Later, Claire watched the girls as they walked across the lawn and up the gently sloping grass toward the house. Brooke, Helen and Sheralyn had separated, but were stopping along the way to chat or hug old friends whom, if it weren't for Garden Club, they would rarely see. Gina, however, plotted a direct course to bypass the tables altogether.

Why did it always seem she couldn't wait to leave?

CHAPTER 8

Gina rolled down the Jeep's window and pulled away from the curb with a painful screech. Her hair whipped frantically about her face as she turned the radio knob until the sound of electric guitars blared from the dash. She began screaming the words of the song at the top of her lungs.

The Barristers lived in an area known as Hillcrest Heights, which was often referred to by outsiders as "the Bubble." The Heights was its own city, surrounded on all sides by Dallas proper, and on a map, the boundaries could be described as round, thus the nickname. Those that lived inside the Bubble enjoyed their independence and there was a feeling of natural selection among its residents. They had their own fire and police departments, city hall and library. Known nationally for its school system, anyone moving to Dallas vied for its landlocked homes and were willing to pay whatever it took to live within its limits.

As she drove through her old neighborhood, Gina allowed her hand to catch the wind outside her window, then took a fast turn west onto Mockingbird Lane. From there, she veered south on Lakeside. Suddenly, the taillights in front of her flashed bright red and she had to stop. A few cars up ahead was a tour bus that was creeping along at twenty miles per hour. Gina was trapped.

Gina glanced off to her right at a small lake that bounded the popular street. Mountains of pink and red azaleas billowed in an unending bank of color and people were everywhere. Frisbee throwers, joggers, dog walkers and a few fishermen were at the water's edge. A young bride was having her picture taken while her stylist and some family members stood in the background, smiling. Gina sighed when, at the end of the street, the bus turned left. She went right.

Gina's first official gardening lesson had been at the breakfast room table after a Saturday morning of helping her father in the yard. They'd been all hot and sweaty and she remembered resting her arms on the round metal table with its bright yellow chairs and looking out at the hot summer day through the windows that surrounded them while he sat next to her. It was where they had most of their interesting conversations.

"Gina," her father suggested, "how about I make us a malted and we sit here and read a little bit about flowers?"

Tony Sessions considered himself to be the master of malted milks. He had dark hair and smiling eyes, a product of Italian grandparents. Every Saturday during the spring and summer, he smelled of fresh cut grass. After he poured the thick malt into a pair of metallic glasses- hers a celery green, his the color of corn- he pushed aside the newspapers with the latest pictures of the war in Vietnam in order to make room for *The Wise Gardening Encyclopedia, 1970*. Pieces of grass were still stuck to the edges of his face.

"Why don't the Worthams and Leedoms work in their yard?" Gina asked, naming off their neighbors. She'd seen the crews of men who came almost every week to the neighbors' yards, or so it seemed.

Thoughtfully, her father flattened the pages of the gardening book.

"That's a very good question," he said. "I think it's because the other daddies have jobs that aren't like mine. They work for other people, and that means they can count on getting a paycheck every week, like clockwork. But I knew a long time ago that I wanted to work for myself. But that means when other people are having trouble making money, I have some of the same trouble. Times are hard these days, with the War, and things getting more expensive. So we get to do our own yard work, but I like it that way, don't you?" She loved the way his eyes crinkled up when he smiled.

Gina had nodded in agreement, but inside she wondered what it would be like to have her Saturdays to watch cartoons all morning like the rest of her friends.

"Let me see, Chapter One," he began that afternoon in the breakfast room, "Dirt." He paused and read silently for a moment. She could tell something had caught his attention.

"Claire," he called toward the kitchen, "it says here we can test our dirt. Run outside and fill a few baggies with dirt. From different spots." His voice was excited and hurried.

"What?" Claire asked, walking in while drying her hands in a dishtowel.

"I'm going to send our dirt off to Texas A & M and they're going to tell us what kind of dirt we've got. Who knows, maybe we're downhill from an old dumping ground. I bet that is why I'm getting scraggly roses and that bush against the garage won't flower."

Gina's mother read over his shoulder for a second.

"That's ridiculous, Tony. We're not downhill from a waste dump or a cemetery and that bush is Indian Hawthorne. It's not worth the two dollars it says you have to send with it. Our problem is you over-water. I have told you that and the yard is telling you that. I've have been learning all about watering and composting at Garden Club and about how varieties are very particular about which side of the house you plant them on and if you would just give me a chance…"

That was Gina's first real lesson in gardening, particularly the part about what happened after the sample results came back along with a letter that said the dirt was fine, that they'd probably just been overwatering. After that, her mother was in charge of the yard.

Before Gina turned thirteen and after the scenes of soldiers on the front page of the newspaper became pictures of long lines at the gas stations, she and her father were in the breakfast room after a Saturday morning of yard work, or hard labor, as her father like to call it. He'd done the mowing and edging and she had raked out the beds. Months of dead leaves had stuffed themselves all fall into every possible cranny beneath the low-growing bushes, packed in so tight they'd become like solid bricks, and the only way to clean them out was to get down on her hands and knees and grab them by the handfuls.

As always, when they were finished, he'd made a blender full of chocolate malt and poured equal amounts into two glasses, setting one in front of her. Gina's cheeks hollowed out as she sucked the thick ice cream through a straw. Finally, she picked up her spoon.

"This is good, Daddy. Aren't you going to drink yours?" He was staring out the bay window at the freshly cut grass. Her mother passed by, and as usual her arms were loaded with sheets and towels, saying nothing, her eyes looking straight ahead. Gina watched her disappear into the garage where the washing machine was. There was a sadness in his beautiful, heavy-lidded eyes.

Suddenly, he roused himself and with a voice she barely recognized he said, "Just remember, Gina, gardening is not for the weak of heart. Things die. Every damn day."

She'd finished her malt alone. A few days later, they had talked to her about the divorce.

CHAPTER 9

"I thought they'd never leave," Mona said, watching the daughters socialize their way across the lawn toward their cars.

"Go? Is it time to leave?" asked Grace.

SueBee stretched herself into her full sitting height and looked around until she saw what she wanted and waved her arm wildly. Claire followed her gaze. Grace's grandson was standing at the dessert table with a small group of young people. She wondered if Gina knew any of them.

Grace's grandson was a handsome young man. He was so helpful and often stepped in when she needed a driver. He was still in school, SMU she thought.

He saw SueBee's waving hand and started toward them.

"Hello, George," Claire said as he went to stand behind his grandmother. "How are you?"

"Fine, thank you, Mrs. Sessions. You?"

"Fine, thank you. We were just discussing how much fun it is to see our children together. How is school?"

"Good. I'm almost done with graduate school."

"How wonderful."

"George, why are you here?" Grace asked.

"He's here to take you home, Grace," said SueBee.

He rested his hands lightly on her shoulders and immediately the tightness between her brows let go and a smile spread across her face. There was a light in her eyes as she looked up at him. She suddenly looked like the old Grace.

"Everyone looks so pretty," said Grace, as if seeing them for the first time. "Is this my cake?" she asked of the untouched piece. "I'm not very hungry."

"That's alright," said SueBee, pushing it away. "Thank you, George. Let us know if there's anything we can do."

"Come on, Grandmother, time to go home."

George carefully helped her up, then held her arm and walked her across the lawn.

An hour later, Mona, SueBee, Charlotte, and Claire were the only ones left, other than the immediate family who had gone upstairs for naps. Ruby and Richard had been sent home with the leftovers. The drapes were drawn, and the rooms felt cool and quiet, as if the house were taking a nap as well. Only an abundance of flower arrangements suggested anyone had died.

"Okay, quick," said Mona, "everyone spread out. Make sure all the glasses and napkins got picked up but I also want to make sure no one is downstairs."

The others nodded and fanned out. In a few minutes, they were back in the kitchen.

"My car's right outside the kitchen door," said Mona. "I think I saw a box of black trash bags in the pantry." SueBee went to look and reappeared with a box of bags.

"Are we ready?" Charlotte said.

The others nodded. Claire was terrified. They looked like bank robbers as they set out in single file toward the silver closet. Suddenly, the door from the dining room swung open, almost knocking SueBee over.

"What are y'all still doing here?" Frank Barrister instinctively tried to right SueBee but didn't notice the black bag she held behind her back. He went to a cabinet by the sink and brought down a jelly jar, and filled it with tap water.

The ladies watched him take a long drink.

"I thought you'd all be gone by now," he said, satisfied.

"We're just about to leave," said Claire. She noticed the glass shaking slightly as he set it down on the counter.

"Is there anything else I'm supposed to do?"

"Not a thing," said Charlotte sweetly. "You go upstairs and relax. We are just about to tidy up a few more things and don't worry if you hear us rattlin' around. We'll be loading up the silver but we'll try to be real quiet."

"Don't worry about me. I'm so tired, I can hardly keep my eyes open." His voice broke as he tried to smile. His tie was gone and Claire saw the scoop of his undershirt, making him look undressed. She realized she'd never seen Frank in less than perfect order.

Charlotte must have felt something, too. "You just need a good nap, honey," she said, taking his elbow. "Someone from

Garden Club will be by to fix dinner for everyone later today. You can't get rid of us yet."

Gently, she led him toward the stairs, her steps matching his bird-like ones, back through the dining room where the table was a shining stretch of mahogany looking even more beautiful now that the lights were off and the heavy draperies closed. At the bottom of the staircase, he lifted a foot, then stopped and turned.

"Thank you, ladies. I don't know what I would have done without you. Louise really loved her Garden Club."

"We know," they chorused from the kitchen, "we loved her, too." Frank continued to move up the steps, looking frail, with Charlotte at his back.

"Finally," said Mona, "I thought he would never leave. Let's get the weed."

CHAPTER 10

Beyond the lake and the big homes and the tour buses was a different world. The landscaping dried up, the houses shrank in size and there were people begging for handouts on most busy corners. This was where Gina reported for duty almost every day.

The party hadn't been that bad. She and the other daughters seemed to have a mutual admiration thing going, especially when they made a united stand against the mothers' typical request for garden club traditions. She'd already forgotten about it when she whipped the car into a parking space in front of a narrow store front that was wedged tightly between a liquor store and a quick cash store.

Rusty's Pawn Shop was antiseptically clean, like a hospital waiting room with eye-jarring white vinyl floors and walls. Two Hispanic women stood hunched over a glass case filled with cell phones as a family with teenagers checked out a wall of electric guitars. Gina hit the small chrome bell on the counter and a man who looked like he lifted weights for a living came out from the back wiping his hands on a towel and smelling of hand sanitizer. As soon as he saw who it was, he grinned, revealing empty spaces in what would have been a million dollar smile.

"Hi, sweetie. How's my favorite cop?" he asked, grinning. Wet carrot-red ringlets fell in his eyes and he threw them back.

"Hi, Rusty, how's my favorite crook?"

"Terrific! What can I do you for?"

"I'm just checking in. Listen, Rusty, I need your help. Remember a few weeks ago I asked you to keep an eye out for certain items?" She watched his eyes but they remained steadily on hers. "I'm still looking for someone trying to pawn really nice ladies' things." Gina looked around the shop. "I know you don't do clothes, but purses, women's jewelry. Have you seen anything? You remember, right?"

"Yeah, I remember," he said, "but I haven't seen anything like that." He leaned over the counter and smiled like a child about to get a present. "Has there been another robbery?"

"You wish. Not since last month, but it's like we're waiting for someone to ask us to dance, just waiting for the next one. And you know it's in my old neighborhood, don't you? I know people who live in there so this one's personal for me. I mean it, Rusty, I'm counting on you to help me out here. There have been six in nine months and it's starting to get embarrassing. Whoever they are, they aren't slowing down. I want to catch them. You'll help me, right?"

Rusty sighed and shrugged like he was feeling her pain. "I'm all out of stolen goods. Sorry."

"What kind of pawn shop is this? The stuff has to go somewhere, right? How could they go nine months and not pawn something?"

"That is a long time." Rusty shook his head. "Sorry. All I got lately are some men's watches and I called it in, honest. You can ask the lieutenant."

Frustrated, Gina leaned against the counter to get a better look at the place. But there was nothing else to see. It could have been any store at the mall. Gina turned back around.

"Thanks, Rusty. Looks like you're getting ready for a competition. Don't hurt yourself."

Gina left the pawn shop and headed for her office, driving south through the maze of Uptown, keeping to the side streets that were lined with trendy shops and condos. Plenty of people were out walking and it was a pleasant day so she rolled down her window. The traffic was slow and the lights at every corner didn't help, but she didn't care. Naturally, at the corner of Maple and Wolf, she caught the red light and just as naturally, glanced over at the patio of Jackson's where there was still a lunch crowd. She saw the bar's owner standing beneath the canopy of Christmas-lit trees at one of the tables. From the way he was waving his arms, she knew he must be in the middle of a good one.

Gina hinged forward over her steering wheel, trying to see who the unlucky audience might be. She could tell it was a man, and the way he kept fighting with his cowlick reminded her of someone.

The car behind her honked his horn so Gina hit the gas, but halfway down the block, she remembered and made an illegal U-turn.

Gina maneuvered the Jeep into Jackson's tiny parking lot behind the restaurant and took what was left of a space between two motorcycles. There was a warped and splintered door directly in front of her that was meant for the staff and regulars, but Gina decided this time she would enter the restaurant the way normal customers did and walked quickly around to the front.

"Gina!" Tom cried, raising both hands in homage. "My hero! Man, you were amazing. Thanks for last night. You don't know how glad I am to get rid of that creep. Reminds me of a story I'm sure I'll think of in just a minute. Gimme five, but what are you doing here?" The sentences landed on top of each other until he noticed the outfit. "You workin' or are you off?"

"Working," said Gina. She slapped his raised hand. "I missed lunch and I'm hungry for one of your greasy cheeseburgers. I thought I might get it to go." She glanced at the man at the table, letting her eyes linger for a moment. He was staring at her as well. She also knew she was right. It was the same guy she'd seen last night, the one who came in from the patio with that girl, then sat in the corner booth and stayed tight. Obviously a couple. His hair looked freshly washed and he kept wrapping it around his ears, then pushing back the cowlick.

Gina blushed when she saw he'd caught her looking. She was definitely thinking how handsome he was. Not pretty like some men, or over-buffed like most of the guys at the station. He was definitely more like a home-cooked handsome, with honest eyes that were stray cat grey and willing to share his thoughts.

"Hi," he said, his eyes travelling over the leather pants before returning to her face. His arms lay relaxed over an open sketchbook.

Gina noticed a tiny white scar that zigzagged across an eyebrow. She decided he was perfect, in a Greek God sort of way, before realizing it was her turn to speak.

"Hello," she said.

He tilted his head slightly, studying her.

"Hi," he said again.

Tom stepped forward. "Oh, sorry. Gina, this is Blake. Blake Downing, meet Gina Sessions. Blake is new to Dallas and thank goodness someone told him about the bar. He's my newest regular."

"Blake," she repeated and then broke her own rules by extending her hand first. His long fingers engulfed hers and naturally, she smiled.

"Why do you look so familiar to me?" he asked. There were spaces between his teeth but of course they matched the grin. Still perfect.

"Ever been arrested?" she asked.

"No." He responded, still studying her face. "No, this was recent." And then he remembered and his eyes widened. "Hey, you were here, at the bar last night."

Gina stopped smiling and felt the color rising in her face. For a second, she'd forgotten.

"You were sitting at the bar and those guys hit on you, and then you left with one. You looked pretty hot," he added, eyeing the glamour boots.

"I was working," said Gina. "I don't normally look like that, or this, like today." She pulled at the black shirt she had on and made a sweeping motion to include the whole outfit. Tom barked a laugh.

"Yeah, she was working alright. She does that occasionally. And she's good, really good."

"Shut up, Tom," Gina said. "I'm a cop, Blake. Last night was business. "

"Seriously?"

Gina raced to change the subject. "I also noticed you were having a pretty intense conversation with a very nice brunette."

Blake thought for a moment. "Oh, that was Harriett, my manager. She's helping me with some shows." Gina looked confused. "I'm a painter," he explained. "She's a nice person."

"Uh huh," Gina said, looking toward the bar.

"You want me to order your regular?" Tom asked.

"Thanks. That would be great."

Gina looked at the sketchbook under Blake's arms.

"Never show a work in progress," he said. "My mother's advice."

He continued.

"They're charcoals for a client. He likes old architecture and my agent was giving me some ideas, places to go see. There's some beautiful stuff in this city."

Gina nodded. "True, especially downtown. There are some very cool houses over in East Dallas. I grew up here and I still stumble across places I've never seen before."

"Like that place across the street."

Gina followed his gaze to the twelve-story Stoneleigh Hotel on the other side of Maple. The entrance to the grand hotel began at the street where a wide walkway flanked by stone lions led up several steps to a huge pair of beveled glass doors. A doorman stood stiffly, wearing a light grey suit and gloves. It was an impressive sight.

They both stared in silence before Blake spoke again.

"Maybe you could show me some of your favorite places?"

His question startled her, but without thinking, she said, "I could do that."

"How about next Saturday?"

Gina's face fell. "I can't. I've got a family thing... with my mom." She was absolutely not going to try to explain a flower show.

"Well, how about afterwards? It doesn't matter how late. Then we can grab something to eat."

Gina didn't have to think long. "Sure."

Tom showed up with a white sack. It had a large grease stain on the side.

"On the house, darlin'. Thanks for last night."

"Thanks. Glad I could help."

"Where should I pick you up?" asked Blake.

She gave him Mona's address. "It's a house in Hillcrest Heights," she said, pointing north. "It's not far from here. Just honk and wait for me outside."

"Just honk?"

"That's the best thing."

Blake shrugged and looked at Tom, who shrugged also. "Okay, if you say so."

Gina turned to go, but then Blake grabbed her hand again, as if to shake it. Their eyes met, and suddenly Gina felt things inside of her that she hadn't felt for a long time.

"I need to get back to work," she choked, pulling her hand away. "Thank you for the burger, Tom, I'll see you next week, have a nice..." Her hip caught the corner of the iron gate and she whimpered in pain, but as both men reached for her, she stumbled backward, mumbling an apology before disappearing around the corner.

It had been one of her worst getaways.

CHAPTER 11

Now that their duties to the Barrister family were taken care of, the ladies had less than a week until the last flower show they would ever have. They woke up Saturday to a perfect day, with just the right amount of cool breeze and sunshine to make a true gardener long to be outside.

Not to be left out of the preparations, Mona's husband Cleeve made sure he'd restocked the birdfeeder in the backyard pecan tree, making it the center of attention for mockingbirds and robins, breathtaking redbirds, and a consistent flow of sparrows fighting for a turn on its tiny wooden shelves. It was a messy tree, like most pecan trees. Its bark looked like lava and the gnarly branches that had survived the ice storms that descended on the city every other year cast themselves outward like the skeletal frame of an umbrella. A fat squirrel hung upside down, clinging to a limb, waiting for his chance to clamber down the chain and have the seed for himself.

Claire and Mona watched all of this in silence from the covered porch outside the kitchen. They sat side by side in two heavy white rockers, sipping iced tea and rocking peacefully, knowing the storm that awaited them inside. There was no need to talk. For just a little longer it would be alright to rock back and forth, in time with one another, and even though they hadn't spoken, they were thinking the same thing. Today was another ending, like saying goodbye to Louise a week ago. The last flower show had finally arrived.

The screen door clapped shut, jarring them both as Cleeve came out, followed by an old yellow Lab at his heels.

"Hello, ladies. I don't think you've ever had a lovelier day for a flower show," he said in his gentlemanly way. "Very different from last year, I'd say. Thought we were going to have to get out the life rafts."

"God must have finally taken pity on us," said Mona, rising to straighten the collar of her husband's golf shirt. "You look very handsome today, Cleeve."

"Thank you. You don't look so bad yourself."

"Which reminds me," she went on, "I don't know if you got a good look at a few of the other members but if you did, I hope you didn't look too surprised."

"What do you mean?"

Mona pulled back on the loose skin around her eyes.

"Oooh, that," Cleeve said. "Sorry, I tried not to stare."

Mona pecked him lightly on the cheek. "Oh well, have a good game." She patted his belly. "Don't let them talk you into more than one beer on the ninth hole."

"I'm not making any promises." He started down the steps.

"I think you should stay and eat dinner at the club," Mona called after him. "We'll probably be congratulating ourselves after this is all over and you know how we like to talk about our husbands."

Cleeve gave her a half-hearted salute while holding tightly to the wooden handrail. The grey-muzzled dog was still following at his heels until halfway down, when Cleeve stopped to give his head a rub. He looked back up at his wife.

"This is the last flower show, right?"

They both nodded.

"No tears?"

Both shook their heads but Claire suspected he didn't believe them. He gave the Lab a final tussle behind the ears and somehow the animal knew to return to his spot on the porch, settling at Mona's feet.

They watched as the car backed slowly out of the garage.

"He's a good one, Mona."

"I think I'll keep him." She checked her watch. "Okay, Claire, eight forty-five. Time to get everyone out."

They both started up out of the rockers, Mona getting to the door first while Claire still struggled with the unstable rocker.

She came back. "Let me help you."

Claire ignored the hand.

"Is it your back?"

"Hip or back, I'm never sure," Claire said, steadying herself with the chair. Mona reached again to take her elbow but she pushed it away.

"I'm alright, Mona. I'm just a little stiff."

"I hope Gina is helping you at home."

"I don't need help at home. I'm fine," said Claire sharply. She hated drawing attention to herself like this. People got a whiff of the slightest little thing and right away started thinking a person was feeble. She wasn't feeble, at least not yet.

"Well then, I hope you'll ask for help when you do need it. That's what daughters are for, you know."

"I don't hear you asking Sheralyn for help."

"What in the world could she possibly help me with? And besides, I have Cleeve."

"I wish you'd be nice to her, Mona. She loves your son and she wants so badly to please you." Claire had made her way to the door by then.

"I don't like people who want to please me. It makes me not want to trust them."

"Mona! That might be the dumbest thing I've ever heard you say. Stop being so proud. And stubborn. You're wasting time, in my opinion."

"Wasting whose time?" Mona asked, following Claire inside.

But Claire didn't have a chance to answer. The kitchen was too noisy, crowded with familiar faces, more than they needed, and there were lots of questions about what needed to be done next for both of them.

As usual, Ruby was focused on keeping things flowing at the sink. Others were busy working with the food, setting out stacks of plates and cutting up fruit. Two men dressed in black were arranging tall crystal champagne glasses on polished trays for the mimosas. One gentleman expertly fanned a stack of napkins with a downturned glass.

At a few minutes before nine, Mona and Claire stood at the front door, Mona with her dark glasses on and her head held high, while the last few members hurried out carrying leftover flowers and supplies. They'd been doing this for almost fifty years and everyone knew she'd disqualify them in a heartbeat if anyone was one minute past nine.

Once they were gone, Claire retrieved the clipboards with the score sheets and together they began the judging in the entryway. The first arrangement had a patriotic theme.

Mona and Claire went room to room and arrangement to arrangement, discussing all the things that by now had become second nature. They knew the rules about construction, height, condition, and all the other things that the Schedule talked about.

The Schedule. For years she'd moaned out loud whenever she'd heard those words, but now she almost had a fondness for the thing. Claire remembered the first time Louise had shown the new club the thick manual of rules for flower shows. It had seemed so thick and each page had narrow margins and was full of black type. There were hardly any pictures. Louise had said it would be their Bible and it had been. Claire hadn't looked at it in years, but she was pretty sure she still knew it by heart.

By now they'd covered the entry, dining room, den and two bedrooms. In the master, Claire watched as Mona checked off items on her checklist as her eyes darted up and down to a nice arrangement in a Chinese porcelain bowl. She looked almost angry, but Claire knew that was her serious face. People who didn't know Mona assumed she was cold and stiff, that she cared more about formality than family. But Claire knew that was not at all true.

The real Mona loved to pull out frozen chicken pot pies and set up folding trays in front of an old TV set where she and Cleeve could spend a rare evening at home watching old movies. They had almost never spent a night apart, and when they did, no matter where in the world they were, they always found a way to call and say goodnight. Theirs was a deep love that they held like a fragile piece of crystal, and only the best of friends were allowed to see it. Claire felt privileged to know that about her friend.

They finished the judging shortly before noon and at the same time, members, daughters and guests had begun to arrive to see the results.

Claire wandered through the house, looking for Gina. Instead she found Brooke, Helen and Sheralyn in the sunroom admiring a lush arrangement of peonies in an antique bowl. It had won a blue ribbon and a large silver tray.

They all looked happy to see her.

"Everything looks so gorgeous. Is Gina here?" asked Brooke.

"Not yet. I assume she's coming," said Claire.

"Oh, I'm sure she is," said Helen, "she wouldn't miss your last show. All the arrangements are beautiful, as always. I can't believe you aren't sad, though."

"Not a bit," said Claire.

"Well, I guess I can understand that. I love coming to the flower shows now but I used to hate them. It was horrible watching Mother run around the house in her pajamas, screaming about 'who took my floral tape' and 'I can't find the perfect container! I have to have the perfect container!' And then afterward, she'd be so relieved. She was so proud of that ribbon. She didn't care what color it was."

Brooke had a shiver. "But just say the words *flower show*, and I break out in hives."

"See!" said Claire. "That's why we can't wait to retire."

"I bet you're going to be bored," said Helen.

"Are you kidding? We have plenty of things to keep us busy."

"I don't think we should let them quit. The food's always so good at these things." At the sound of Gina's voice, Claire turned.

"Gina," Claire said, and then was speechless.

Her daughter had on a pale grey silk suit that shimmered when she moved. The jacket was cut at the waist and with the perfect amount of flair that exaggerated her hourglass shape. Her hair was pulled back in a tight bun. Sophisticated was the word that came to mind. And then Claire noticed she was even wearing hose. She knew better than to say anything about that.

"Wow, Gina, you look great," said Sheralyn. "I love that suit."

"Beautiful," said Charlotte, clearly impressed. She had just found their group.

"Obviously no one thinks I know how to dress."

"Just say thank you," said Helen. "You look fabulous."

"Thank you," said Gina, obediently.

Chimes rang out as one of the catering staff trailed between the rooms with a tiny xylophone.

Brooke placed an arm around Helen. "Let's go find your mom. See you all in there."

Claire watched them go, then turned her attention back to Gina, looking her over again. "I just can't get over how beautiful you look. I'm so proud of you."

"What?"

"I'm just so relieved."

"Relieved about what?"

"Oh nothing. Let's go in. I want to get a good seat."

They sat at a table for eight. It was Claire, SueBee, Charlotte and Mona, along with their daughters. Everyone talked at the same time during the consommé and salad course, but by the time the main course had arrived, the mothers were doing more listening than talking, and the conversation had turned to more serious things. A child with learning differences, a husband's problem at work, and more than a few sincere questions about something shared the last time they'd been together.

Claire was content to watch. The daughters looked beautiful, each in her own unique way, and she felt moved as their girls talked about feeling old and who was seeing wrinkles and who had the most grey in their hair. They teased Sheralyn because she was so much younger and Gina laughed at being teased herself. She hadn't seen Gina laugh in a long time. Claire's heart filled with love for them all.

Claire wanted to say something but it would have ruined things. She wanted to tell them that they'd felt and said almost exactly those same things to their own mothers fifty years ago and now they'd become like sisters, all different, not always friends, but always, always there for each other. She wanted to warn them not to waste what the mothers had begun, this gift of friendship that had been handed to them, literally on a silver platter. If they didn't nurture it, it would surely die. But Claire couldn't say anything. She didn't know how to say it and it was definitely not the right time.

If there had not been Garden Club, this is what I would have missed, Claire thought, her eyes glassy with tears, *not the flower shows or meetings, or that silly Christmas exchange.* She wondered if it were possible that something so special as Garden Club was about to die.

Gina suddenly looked at her watch and stood up.

"Sorry, guys, I lost track of time. I've got to go. Thank you so much for lunch, Mona, I loved the flower show. It was so good to see you guys." She smiled at everyone and Claire could tell she meant it.

"Are you going back to work?" asked Charlotte.

"No, I promised to help a friend who just moved here."

"Who?" asked Claire.

"You don't know him, Mom. Nice to see everyone," said Gina. "This was fun. Hope to see you guys again soon."

"We should do lunch," said Sheralyn.

The mothers and daughters watched in silence as she left the room.

"She's leaving from the front door," SueBee whispered. "Must be special. And she said 'him,' Claire. Do you know anything about a *him*?"

"No idea," said Claire, shaking her head.

"I'm sorry, but I can't stand it," said Helen, jumping up from the table. Everyone followed her out of the dining room and to the living room. They divided themselves between the front windows and pushed back the draperies to see.

"Whose car is that?" asked SueBee, watching Gina walk toward a parked car.

"I don't know. Can you see whose driving?"

"What kind of car is that?" said Claire. "He should have come to the door."

"It looks like a nice car."

"Who is that?"

"Oh, Claire, it's the nineties. It's not a big deal."

"There they go," said SueBee.

Claire backed away from the window, looked up, and pressed her hands together.

"Thank you, Jesus."

CHAPTER 12

Mona's house felt naked with the arrangements gone. Like the seven dwarfs, the flower show committee had moved all the furniture back into place and put the silver back into Mona's spacious silver closet. Boxes of place cards and ribbons, easels, and signs had been stacked by the kitchen door. Unlike the arrangements and the silver, no one was quite sure where they should go.

Claire and Charlotte propped their bare feet on the big coffee table in Mona's den and SueBee tucked her toes beneath her bottom on the couch. Mona walked in with a bottle of pinot.

As soon as she'd poured, SueBee raised her glass. "I'm makin' a toast..."

"Hallelujah," Mona finished for her, drinking deeply.

"Cheers."

"Cheers."

SueBee acted bullied then gave up and drank.

The clock chimed three on the mantle and Cleeve's dog shifted in his sleep beneath the coffee table.

"Ladies, we done good," said Mona. "It was a wonderful ride. Now on to spending our days travelling, meeting for stimulating conversation, and taking care of our friends."

"So let's talk business," said SueBee. "None of us are getting any younger. We might as well go ahead and divide the silver up among the girls."

"I agree," said Charlotte, "it's not doing us any good just sitting in our closets. We might as well give it to them and hopefully they'll put it to good use. I hope our grandchildren will be having their own showers and parties someday."

"Shouldn't we try to keep track of it? Are we really just giving them a certain piece? I think we should write up a contract or something."

"You can't manage it from the grave, Claire," said Charlotte. "It'll be nice to have more room in my closet, though."

"Except I don't have a silver closet," said Claire.

"What do you think, Mona?" SueBee asked.

"I hate the idea of just handing it over. That's way too easy for them. However, on the other hand, if we wait much longer, we're going to forget who has what and it might get lost. And once we're gone, you know they'll put everything in a garage sale." The others nodded in agreement. "Probably give it away." She shuddered into her drink.

"I say we just give it to them," said Charlotte. "We don't really need it anymore. By the way, summer's coming. Anyone else want to take a trip? How's the checking account, Claire?"

"It's fine."

"I've never been to Branson," suggested SueBee.

"Branson is for old people," said Claire.

"You are old, dummy," said Mona. She seemed more relaxed than earlier.

"We are old," corrected Charlotte.

"Old farts," said Mona.

"I would like to think of us as experienced, not old farts," said SueBee. "And I want to go on a trip. Claire, pick someplace and just let us know."

Claire nodded. Since she was the Club's treasurer, she usually got put in charge of organizing ways to spend their money. It was almost like spending her own money, which she didn't usually have.

Claire tilted the bottle over her glass, then added to Charlotte's. She thought again how beautiful her friend was with her long slender arms and a dancer's legs. Even now they were crossed at the ankle. It was just like Charlotte to always do things so perfectly.

Suddenly, Charlotte popped up from the couch and with her glass in hand, she began strolling around the room like a visitor would, passing Mona's collection of Staffordshire and Japanese jade trees until she came to a stop at a bookshelf of six identical trophies. She leaned in closely to read the tiny brass plaques that were screwed to their bases.

They were not elaborate pieces. Far from it. They were smallish blocks of black granite topped with a gold bowl and spilling out of each bowl were rounded shapes suggesting flowers.

Charlotte took a sip of her wine while an arm draped casually across her small belly.

Watching her, Claire asked, "What is it, Charlotte?"

She ignored her or didn't hear. Claire was about to repeat herself when Charlotte picked up one of the trophies, whirled around and marched back to the couch and thrust the object in front of them.

"The Excelsior," she announced.

"Yes, that is our little bobble of a trophy. What about it?" asked Mona.

"The-Ex-cel-si-or," she repeated, separating each syllable.

No one understood.

Frustrated, Charlotte picked up a pair of reading glasses from a basket on the table, looked closely at the label and began to read from the brass plaque.

"Excelsior Award, Hillcrest Heights Garden Club, Dallas County Garden Center flower show..."

"Thank you, Charlotte, but we know what it says," SueBee said.

"We are missing one," Charlotte emphatically. "There should be another one on that shelf."

"Oh, my gosh, Charlotte. Please, do not remind me," said Mona.

"They cheated! Remember? We all knew it. We should have won and there should be another trophy on that shelf. That's all I'm saying."

'They' were the Goldenrods, a much younger gardening club who'd appeared out of nowhere and won the trophy. It had been humiliating.

"I was so mad," SueBee said, remembering. "They brought in that tacky designer from California."

"That was so unfair," said Claire.

"I wanted to kill someone," said Mona.

"I think we should win it back," said Charlotte.

"What?" Mona asked. The dog, who'd been quietly snoring beneath the coffee table, suddenly raised his head to look at her.

"It's this month and I think we should enter. We win, and then there will never ever *ever* be another need to do another flower show again," declared Charlotte.

They were all speechless.

"Oh come on, one last time, it'll be fun," said Charlotte, sitting on the edge of the couch with a ballerina's posture. "Please."

The Excelsior Award was a part of The Excelsior Flower Show, the biggest flower show in Texas. It was held every five years by the State Garden Club Association at the Dallas Convention Center and Hillcrest Heights had started entering years ago. It had been Louise's idea. And then they'd won. For twenty-five years, the Hillcrest Heights Garden Club had brought home the grand prize, a four-foot-tall trophy that Mona kept in her garage until the end of the year when it got traded in for the midget versions that now populated her shelf.

"The Excelsior is not fun," said Mona.

"It's only a few weeks away," Claire hinted softly, not wanting to hurt Charlotte's feelings.

"Why in the world would we enter the Excelsior?" asked Mona.

"Because we can win. We can do flower arrangements blindfolded so who cares if it's only a few weeks away? Let's show those bimbos who the real champions are. I don't want to retire letting them think they beat us. Do you?"

"But they did beat us," said Claire, remembering the way the Goldenrods had screamed and started crying. It had been humiliating.

"Well, they did have that designer from California in a van out in the parking lot churning out arrangements," said SueBee.

"See," said Charlotte, "we'll make sure they don't do that again and I know we can win."

"Charlotte, you've obviously had too much to drink," said Mona. "I've hung up my clippers and honestly, I don't know what I'd do to them if I were in the same room as *The Goldenbitches*. Reading about them in the Living section of the newspaper is bad enough."

"We'd probably lose anyway, and how embarrassing would that be?" Claire added, speaking into her wine before taking a sip.

Claire continued. "Brooke told me just the other day what a big club they are. They keep adding members and they're young. Not that that means anything, but Gina told me after the flower show this morning that she heard someone say they thought our arrangements looked dated."

"Wait a minute," said Mona, staring at Claire. "Are you saying we *can't* win?"

"What? No, I didn't say that."

"Do you think that because we are old and outnumbered that we can't win?

"Well, maybe they're right. It's true, isn't it? We're old and maybe we've lost our touch. And besides, I've always thought the scoring had something to do with body type. The Goldenrods are all very skinny."

"Charlotte," Mona barked to her elegant friend, her hair colored a light brown with blond highlights, "I agree. We are going to enter the competition and win back the Excelsior."

"Oh, for pity's sake," said Claire in disbelief, "you just said that to spite me. It's all ridiculous."

Charlotte clapped her hands victoriously and flopped back on the couch.

"But how, Mona?" said SueBee. "We don't have enough members anymore. But then again, maybe if we got our own designer...?"

"I have a better idea," said Mona.

"What?" said SueBee.

"What?" asked Charlotte.

"Mona?" asked Claire, worried by the look in her eyes.

"We get the daughters to help us."

There was a moment of silence.

"I think someone else has also had way too much to drink," said SueBee.

"If they each do one or two arrangements, we will win by sheer numbers. We might even win a few categories." Mona's eyes sparkled.

"I hate to be a realist," said Claire, already feeling guilty, "but they aren't going to help us. Why would they? And they really don't know anything about flower arranging."

"They won't be doing it by themselves," insisted Mona. "We'll teach them."

SueBee rubbed her temples. "Claire's right, Mona. They always say they're too busy. I think the wine is giving me a headache."

Mona's smile widened, and she raised a finger.

"Ahhh, but you haven't heard my idea. We have a secret weapon." She paused, enjoying the suspense. "They want the silver, right?"

Seconds passed. The dog settled over on his side. Suddenly SueBee's eyes opened wider, the corners of her mouth turning up.

"Do you think they'll do it for the silver?"

"They help us win back the Excelsior, we give them the silver. I think they'll love it."

Charlotte sat up straight. "Actually, that might work. No wonder we let you be president so often."

"I'm sorry, but I still don't think they'll do it," said Claire.

"Maybe Gina won't, but I bet the others will."

"Maybe she will, if the others agree," said SueBee, sympathetically. "You never know. I would tell her how much it would mean to you. And if she still says no, then we'll manage without her."

They obviously did not know her daughter, thought Claire. Sometimes she didn't either but it made her sad, imagining all the other daughters, jumping in to help, dividing up the silver. What if Gina never got even a single piece? Claire thought of her favorite pieces, the ones with her name inscribed on them. It would take a miracle to get Gina to go along with the plan. Thankfully, the others had another idea.

"Maybe if we put them all in the same room and explain how *extremely* important it is to us..." began Charlotte.

"Exactly," interrupted Mona, "we put them all in the same room and make them feel really, really guilty. I do it all the time."

Everyone thought for a moment.

"Actually, that might work," Charlotte said.

CHAPTER 13

When asked, Gina would say she was *very* happy. She stayed busy, loved her job, and visited her mother at least once a week. She went to church on Sundays and tried to eat healthy, but she would be the first one to admit that everything she did was either written on a piece of paper or the mental list in her mind. She was good at making lists and checking them off made her feel good, at least at the time. But every day needed its list, and at the end of the day, all she had were check marks. Some days Gina caught herself wondering what was missing. She'd catch a glimpse of a hairline crack in the armor that protected her from fear and worry and the 'what ifs'. She'd wonder if she was doing something, or not doing something that one day she would regret. All she could do was wait for more information. Until then, she would try not to look at the cracks.

Gina was relieved to see Blake's brown Volvo waiting for her at the curb, just as instructed.

"Hi," she said, putting on her seatbelt, staring straight ahead.

"Nice house."

"Most of my mom's friends have nice houses."

"You know a bunch of people are watching us, right?"

Without looking, Gina stared straight ahead. "Of course they are. Go that way."

The car pulled forward and they drove in silence for a few minutes.

"So, where are you from?"

"Originally? Minnesota."

"That's a long way away. What brought you here?"

"My grandmother. She moved here as a young bride from Europe with my grandfather. My parents are both gone and she's a tough old German, but I decided I should be closer. So I found a new agent and moved."

Gina turned to look at him for the first time. "My mother lives alone, not too far from here. Sometimes I think about moving away, but it's not really an option. She doesn't think she needs me, but I know she does."

He changed the subject. "Do you like being a police officer?"

"A detective," she corrected him, "and yes, I love it. It's all I ever wanted to do. Turn here," she said, suddenly throwing up a finger and pointing right. Blake veered right, taking them further south and east. The neighborhood was very different as they drove past blocks of boarded up apartment buildings and empty playgrounds until they came to a wide boulevard with a grassy median and tall mansions on both sides of the street.

The stately homes had been built in the '20s and for years had provided visual entertainment for the latest generation of joggers, dog-walkers, and trim mothers pushing toddlers along the sidewalk in colorful strollers.

"Swiss Avenue," Gina announced. Blake slowed the Volvo. "It's one of the oldest neighborhoods in Dallas."

He stopped in front of a red-bricked mansion. Concrete benches and flowering beds sat beneath the trees. Everything was meticulously maintained.

"That's beautiful. I need to bring my sketchbook next time." He leaned across her to look out her window. His head was inches from her face and she could smell his powdery cologne. Gina pressed herself back into her seat, afraid he might brush against her shirt. She held her breath and stared at his head until he was upright again.

"Okay?" He looked curiously at her.

Gina stared into his eyes, then at his mouth. "What?"

"I asked if you thought it would be okay if I took a few pictures?" She nodded. He got out of the car, pulled a large camera from the trunk, and began shooting pictures. Gina wiped her palms against the fabric upholstery.

Once he was back in the car, Blake followed her directions to another part of town.

Little Mexico was a forgotten neighborhood. It was tucked away on a busy street that led into downtown, separated from the cars that flew by every day on their way to work by a thick, low wall that had once been yellow but was now a dirty grey. The stucco houses of the same color blended into the wall, and there was a hint of red in the clay tile roofs.

"This is a real neighborhood with families who have lived here for generations," said Gina. "There used to be mostly bars across the street but they've closed." She pointed far away. "Behind that is an abandoned steel mill. Now it's surrounded by new construction and empty lots.

Blake pulled to the curb across the street.

"It's like another country," he said, looking at the men and women, some old, some young, seated in plastic chairs on the front stoops of the low slung bungalows, laughing and talking as their children darted among them, shouting in a language they couldn't understand.

"That's why they call it Little Mexico," Gina reflected.

Blake raised his camera and took a few pictures. They drove on, then stopped for coffee at a diner that had leather booths and tables with formica tops.

"Have you been painting long?" she asked.

"Feels like all my life."

Gina thought for a moment, then asked, "I hope you don't mind my asking, but how old are you?"

"Twenty-nine. How old are you?"

"Thirty-three."

He smiled. "Glad we got that over with."

The waitress brought their coffee. Gina held hers with both hands. She tried to relax but still was distracted every time she looked at him.

"Do you go to church?" she asked. Immediately she wished she could swallow her tongue.

"When I can."

"What does that mean?" She stared at her coffee, biting her lip. She sensed him shifting in the booth.

"If you're asking me if I'm a Christian, then yes. If..."

"Sorry." Gina suddenly stopped him. "I can be a little too direct sometimes."

"Why does that not surprise me?" Blake looked at his watch. "Oh, look at the time. I promised my grandmother I'd take her to the store."

"That bad?" said Gina.

"Not bad at all. I really did tell my grandmother I'd take her to the store."

They both smiled awkwardly.

CHAPTER 14

Monday morning, the message light was already blinking on Gina's answering machine when she stepped out of the shower. Reluctantly, she tapped the play button.

"Hello, Gina, are you there? Helloooooo," her mother's voice sang. "Did you have fun after the flower show? Just curious but I'd love to hear. Do I remember you saying something about going in early? Well, never mind, but I need for you to be at Mona's house *this* Friday at ten a.m. Not next Friday, *this* Friday. It's e*xtremely* important and if you don't have time you don't have to stay for lunch but all the daughters are coming and when you come, please don't... oh, never mind. But please, honey, don't be late. Please... beep." And then the machine cut her off.

Gina didn't need to call her back. Even if she wanted to, there was nothing to report. Blake hadn't called since their tour of the city on Saturday. She made a mental note to write the Friday meeting on her calendar, wondered briefly what the mothers were up to and then put it out of her mind.

Gina stayed busy all week. She would have forgotten about the Friday meeting except that there was a message on her machine that morning to remind her.

"Hello, Richard," Gina said, entering Mona's kitchen. "I know, I'm late. Have they started?"

He nodded in the direction of the living room as he polished someone's silverware, warning her with a look.

"They just got quiet. You better go on in. They're up to something."

Gina stepped quickly to the living room where Mona stood behind a pop-up podium that belonged to the club. The garden club members were already seated in the green folding chairs they used for large meetings and about twenty daughters sat on the other side of the room in folding chairs as well.

From the doorway, Gina could see everyone. The mothers— Claire was up close near Mona—were seated on one side while the daughters were seated on the other. Obviously, the teams had already been decided. Gina was relieved to see an empty chair on the last row, closest to the door. She remembered she was chewing gum and made a mental note to not chew.

Mona cleared her throat. "Good morning, everyone," she began from the front of the room. She checked her note cards, hesitated slightly, and Gina noticed the cards fluttered. She'd never seen Mona nervous before.

"Good morning, everyone," Mona recited, this time from her cards, "we are so happy to have our daughters and daughters-in-law with us today." She paused to allow time for the mothers to clap.

Gina leaned forward toward Sheralyn, who was sitting in the row in front of her.

"Why are we here?"

Sheralyn cupped a hand over her mouth and whispered back, "No idea. Mona sent my invitation in the mail, didn't say another word."

"We've gathered you here for a very exciting announcement," Mona continued.

"Passing down the silver, I hope," Sheralyn said, grinning back at Gina.

"I hope everyone enjoyed our *final* flower show as much as we did. We are proud of our years together, how much we've learned, and the contributions we've made to Dallas through our volunteer hours and our participation in a myriad of projects like the State Fair flower show or the Children's Garden at the downtown park." Mona paused. "So many things to be proud of, don't you all agree? I also think I'm speaking for everyone when I say we are extremely happy to be retiring from having that little old flower show." Many of the members nodded when Mona glanced up, smiling. "But ladies, I don't believe it's time to hang up our clippers. We have one more thing on our bucket list."

"They have a bucket list?" Gina whispered to Sheralyn, who shrugged.

Mona smiled toward the mothers' side of the room, then turned to face the girls. Gina accidentally swallowed her gum.

"For many, *many* years, the whole state of Texas has known that the Hillcrest Heights Garden Club *owned* the Excelsior." Her voice suddenly became cold. "We won the Excelsior every five years. It was our tradition." She was no longer reading from the cards as she gripped the edges of the podium. "You girls remember us talking about the Excelsior, don't you?" Several heads on the daughters' side bobbed rapidly.

Gina quietly moaned. Stories of the Excelsior could go on for hours. They'd been blown up into such tall tales, she didn't know what to believe. The Excelsior was like the Holy Grail, in all its gaudy, four-foot-tall monstrosity glory, made of cheap metal that sat for a year in Mona's garage, then got traded in for a midget replica that went on a shelf in Mona's den.

Gina vaguely remembered something bad happening at the last show. Whatever it had been, it was like the world had come to an end. According to the mothers, the *Goldenrods*—they always said it with a sneer—had cheated, and since Gina had just become a cop, they all expected her to do something about it. But there was nothing she could do because no one could actually prove a crime had been committed, which did not please the mothers.

"Girls," Mona spoke loudly from the front, "we've decided that we can't retire with the stain of losing the Excelsior undeservedly. We are going to win it one last time." She gripped the edges of the podium and gave it a kick, turning it to face the daughters. "We are asking for your help. We need every single one of you girls to make an arrangement. Maybe two. We don't have as many members as we used to and there's no way we can get enough points to win without you."

Somehow, Mona found a way to lean even further over the podium. "We need you to help us win the Excelsior one more time, and preferably before we die."

The room was silent. Gina heard an oven door slam shut in the kitchen and it sounded like someone had just flushed the toilet down the hall.

Sheralyn's hand slowly went up. Mona nodded permission. "Mona, I'm sorry, but I don't think I can. My schedule is already packed with the children's activities, Billy has so many games, and..."

"Hush, Sheralyn," Mona said. "Anyone else?"

Brooke indicated she would like to speak and again, Mona nodded her permission. Unlike Sheralyn's attempt, Gina felt a sense of relief knowing Mona respected Brooke's strong-mindedness.

"Mona, I don't think we would be any help. We don't even know how to do an arrangement."

At the word *help*, Charlotte leapt to her feet. "But we'll teach you! We'll give you as many lessons as you want. We have four weeks, I think?" No one said anything. "Please? It would mean so much to us."

"Mom, we can't. Sorry," said Brooke.

"You could if you wanted to," said Mona.

Gina raised her hand.

"Yes?" said Mona.

"We don't want to. It's a nice bucket list but it's not our bucket list. I'm afraid you're on your own." Gina was sure she saw herself in every eye.

SueBee gripped the back of a chair and used it to slowly stand up.

"We were afraid you might say that. So let us put it to you this way." She looked toward the kitchen and naturally, everyone followed her gaze as she gave a regal wave.

It was a cue. Those members that could walk without assistance had been standing outside the doorway and began entering the room in single file. They were all preciously old but still steady on their feet, and each one held her head high like a proud peacock. Staring straight ahead, they each carried a piece of the Club's silver collection. Some were carrying two.

The solemn parade entered the room. They wound between the chairs so that everyone could see, and then, as if someone had poked a hole in a balloon, the tension that had been filling the room seeped away, replaced by a giddy feeling. These were proud women and there was so much glittering, sparkling silver. Gina wasn't sure if she was inspired by the women or the silver or both, and when they were leaving the room and on their way back to the silver closet, SueBee said in her soft Southern voice, "One arrangement, one piece of silver."

Sheralyn's hand shot into the air. "I'll do it!"

Brooke and Helen, sitting a few rows ahead of Gina, raised their hands, too. Gradually there was a sea of hands on the daughters' side of the room. Only Gina's hand remained in her lap.

"Thank you, girls, we really do appreciate it," said Mona. "We'll work out a schedule to teach you everything we know. Four weeks is not a lot of time, but if we start right away, it's possible. Barely."

"Unbelievable," said Gina, under her breath. She looked toward the kitchen.

"Well then, that's settled. We should take care of a few items of business."

While Mona talked, Gina slipped out of her chair and backed into the hallway. She would say goodbye to Ruby then leave, but in the hallway, half-way between the living room and kitchen, she saw old Mrs. Childress coming out of Mona's silver closet. The old woman hurried down the hallway without noticing that the door to the closet had not closed properly.

Gina pushed the door closed, but it refused to catch and swung open again. She tried wiggling the knob, but again, it wouldn't latch. Instead, it creaked open and as it did, a dim light came on inside. Gina went inside.

Mona's silver closet was the size of a large bathroom. The smell of silver polish and old wood filled the small room. Polishing cloths lay folded on the shelves and on one side was what appeared to be the family silver while on the other side was the Club's collection. Gina walked slowly along the shelves, her fingers following the hard edge of one of them. She read off the engraved names on the sides of silver bowls and in the hollows of the trays. Several appeared more than once, and sometimes, on the same piece. When she saw her mother's name, she couldn't help but smile.

Reaching the closet's end, Gina noticed there was a second, smaller door. She tried the knob, assuming it was for more storage but when she opened the door, the smell of marijuana sent her nose hairs tingling. She ducked her head but not enough and hit the low sill. Rubbing her head, Gina entered the inner space. In a moment, her eyes had adjusted with the help of several skylights. That's when she recognized the white tubes snaking in a graceful pattern from floor to ceiling with marijuana plants bursting from small circles every few inches. The air felt wet and she noticed misters puffing away from tubes hanging from the ceiling.

Gina's heart pounded inside her chest as her mind struggled to comprehend what she was seeing. She backed out of the room, hitting her head again, and tried not to touch anything until she could close the door with her foot. She leaned against the shelves, rubbing her head, trying to think who or what was doing this to Mona. Someone had obviously found a way to sneak in, and was using Mona's silver closet to grow marijuana and she had the horrible thought it might be one of Mona's boys. She'd always thought they were destined for prison, one way or another. She remembered them at the family picnics, sneaking beers and smoking behind the barn. Bryan, Sheralyn's husband, had always been the kind one, but the others had been crazy. Now she had to go tell Mona.

Gina retraced her steps through the silver closet, but as she did, she noticed a different shelf. She'd missed it on her way in, possibly because it was much lower and raw, not like the others that were lined in the same blue silver cloth. There was a simple basket lined with a red-checkered kitchen towel, filled with several plump baggies of dried marijuana. Her hands were trembling as she slowly opened a small wooden box beside it and picked from a stack of Polaroid photographs.

The first picture showed two women in a hospital room. One, the patient, sat on a narrow bed, high off the ground, with a dozen pill bottles on a bedside table beneath bright lights. She looked feeble, almost at death's door, but she was smiling broadly. Sitting next to her was a familiar figure, whose face was obscured by a strategic cloud of smoke. The patient held a tiny marijuana cigarette.

Gina picked up another photograph, and then another, and though each was of a different patient, the bedside friends appeared in more than one. In each one, their faces were always hidden in a cloud of smoke. Gina looked closer.

Her foot kicked something soft beneath the shelves. She leaned down and saw several grocery bags, all stapled closed and each one decorated with a happy face and date.

"Mona!" Gina barked seconds later from the back of the living room.

Madam President was clearly annoyed at the interruption, and then she recognized the baggie Gina was dangling in the air. One whole side of the room gave a collective gasp.

"I saw the pictures, too. What is this?" Gina asked, giving the baggie another shake.

Mona looked over her dark glasses. "It's weed, of course, and it belongs to the Club. Please go put it back where you found it."

"I know what it is. But what is it doing in your silver closet?"

"What is that?" Sheralyn asked.

"Oh dear," said Charlotte, her hand covering her mouth. She looked between Mona and Gina, then settled on Mona.

Claire turned in her chair to face her daughter .

"Gina, it's alright. I know you might not understand, but it really is for medicinal purposes." She looked hopefully around the room. "And I think they are going to make it legal someday anyway." Several heads nodded.

"You know about this, Mom?"

"Please, Gina, just put it back. It has nothing to do with the Excelsior. It belongs to the Club." Claire turned back around.

"Who cares about the Excelsior, Mom? What are you doing with this? At your age!"

"Do you know about this, Mom?" Helen asked.

"Of course I do," SueBee said.

"Gina, can we please get back to our meeting?" began Mona.

"No, we can't. You need to explain this."

"Oh, Gina, we're not going to explain anything right now," Claire said. "Just please, let Mona finish the meeting. We can explain everything later. It's all very innocent. Mona, go ahead. Finish what you were saying about the first lesson."

"I don't know what to say. I could be arresting..." Gina began again, then stopped. All eyes were on her. "Okay, wait a minute. Now listen to me." She looked around the room and realized she had everyone's attention. "You want something from us? Well, no one is going to help you win back the Excelsior, *unless*—and I mean it—unless you empty out that closet now."

"No," Mona said. "That is a private endeavor that is used for the benefit of others. And we've already made a deal for the Excelsior. You've agreed to help in exchange for the silver. This other thing, that's not part of the deal."

Gina lowered her voice. "This is not up for discussion." She looked at her mother. "You know I have to do *something* about this, don't you?"

"She has a point, Mona," Claire said.

Mona looked like she was about to explode and stared at Gina through narrowed eyes.

"The Excelsior for the weed," confirmed Gina.

Finally, Mona nodded.

"But we still get the silver, right?" Sheralyn said. The others had forgotten about the silver.

"I don't care about the silver," Gina said. "But Sheralyn's got a point." She sat down, then stood up again, "the sooner the better."

"Hold your horses," Mona said, waving her hand. "First of all, we can't just quit today. A lot of people depend on us."

"That's true," SueBee said.

"Assisted living is bad enough without a little weed," came a small voice from somewhere on the mothers' side.

Gina almost fell getting out of her chair. "You're selling this?" Several grey heads bobbed up and down. "Oh, no! Please don't tell me this is in more than one closet?"

Several heads bobbed.

"How many?" Gina counted at least six hands, then struggled to find her voice. "Ladies, I don't care who, what, when, where, or why, but you're going to shut down every single closet and hand over the silver. If you don't, then, then...I'll have to arrest all of you."

"That's not fair," Charlotte said.

"Mother!" Brooke said.

"Would you really?" Claire asked her daughter.

"How badly do you want that trophy?"

Seconds passed, until finally Mona let out a long breath.

"Oh, alright," she said through clenched teeth. "But you girls can't just enter the contest. We have to win."

Gina's eyes darted to Claire, who mouthed, "Take the deal."

"Really?" Gina said.

"Yep," Mona said, leaning again over the podium.

Gina looked from Brooke to Helen then Sheralyn. All nodded. "Okay."

Sheralyn reached out and took Gina's hand. "Oh good. Does that mean you're going to do an arrangement, too?"

"I guess so." Gina said, stuffing the weed into a pocket and sitting back down. "Among other things."

At the front, Mona adjusted her glasses and fluffed her hair. "Now, SueBee, thank God we can finally move on. Will you please pass out the *Schedules*?"

SueBee left the room and returned wheeling a cart stacked high with cardboard boxes and began handing out thick white manuals to all the daughters.

"We did *not* make extras and you should bring them with you to every meeting. It has all the rules and regulations for participating in a standard flower show." She held one up but not for long because it was so heavy. "For the next four weeks, ladies, this is your Bible."

CHAPTER 15

"How in the world are we gonna' teach them everything they need to know about flower arrangin' in less than four weeks?" asked SueBee in a soft drawl. Whenever she had something important to say, her Louisiana accent came through.

It was the following Monday morning and they were seated around Mona's kitchen table. SueBee bounced the eraser end of a pencil on an open calendar as Claire and Charlotte studied their own. A pot of hot tea and a plate of ginger snaps sat off to the side. Claire had already asked about Cleeve in case they needed to talk about the you-know-what, and Mona had explained that he had already been in and out of the kitchen for his breakfast.

"And don't forget," said Claire, "that's just the half of it. Everyone has to clean out their closets. Let me know if you need help."

"We have to tell everyone," SueBee said, dropping her pencil. "All those sweet people at The Village. They're going to be so upset. I don't want to be the one to tell them. Mona, you're going to have to do it."

"Try to tell them in a positive way," said Charlotte. "Tell them we'll find someone to take our place, they won't be without it for long and that we'll do our best to keep them happy."

"You can't say that, Charlotte. Where are we going to find someone to take our place?" asked Claire. "Church? That's our only other group of friends."

"I don't know. We can ask around," she said.

"Really?" Mona said. "You want to ask around at church?"

"This is my fault," said Claire. "I'm so sorry. She shouldn't have been in there."

"Oh, Claire, it's not your fault. You should be proud of her, standing up to us the way she did," said SueBee. "I wasn't sure who was going to win that fight. She was impressive."

"She was a pain in the ass," said Mona. "I should have kept a lock on that door."

"I am proud of her," said Claire, surveying the others, then added quietly, "but it does make things a little complicated."

SueBee picked up her pencil again. "If everyone will bring their weed over to my house we can box it up and deliver it. It should last them a long time. As for the equipment, I think I'm going to store everything in my garage. You never know what that tubing might be good for."

Charlotte and Claire nodded but Mona looked unhappy.

"I don't think so. I think we should hold off until after the flower show," said Mona. "Remember, I said the girls have to help us win the trophy. So if we don't win, I'm not shutting down."

"Hah," spouted Claire, "she's not going to like that. She takes her job very seriously. I don't think it matters that we're family." She wrapped her arms tightly around herself and sighed loudly. "I wish she had never found it."

Mona looked down at her calendar. "Well, we will just have to see. Now, let's get started. We need to put some dates on the calendar."

Claire sighed again.

"Oh, what is it, Claire?"

Claire was a sigh-er. Sometimes her thoughts and feelings escaped her mouth without her even knowing. "Nothing," she said, forcing a smile.

"I don't believe you," said Charlotte.

"Nothing," she said more insistently, then opened her calendar and re-arranged herself in her seat.

Charlotte touched her arm. "It's alright, Claire, it's not your fault she's a police officer. She is just doing her job. We'll figure this out."

"Of course, I just have a few little worries about what I'm going to do."

"Oh, come on, Claire, for heaven's sake, what is it exactly that you don't know? You don't have a closet," said SueBee.

Claire chose her words carefully. "I was thinking, what if you moved everything out of your closets, but instead of dumping it, you take it somewhere else? Maybe we could rent some space down in Deep Ellum, or near the airport? Lots of places could work, and then we could tell the girls we changed our minds, and don't care about the Excelsior anymore. And then that's it, we're in the clear. We won't have to tell the girls and we can still give them the silver if we want, but we keep the business going. We will just have to be a little more cautious."

"Where did that come from?" asked Mona.

"You think we could keep that secret?" asked SueBee.

"I don't want to lie to Brooke," said Charlotte. "I was fine as long as she didn't know, but now she does and she's going to ask. I just couldn't lie to her."

"That's not a problem for me," said Mona, "but you're saying we don't even try to win back the Excelsior? You think we should just pass out the silver without making them do anything to earn it?"

"Who cares about the trophy or passing on the silver?" said Claire, her voice rising. "It's a piece of metal, it'll go on a shelf, Mona, in your perfect house, and someday, like everything else we own, it will be sold at a garage sale. I bet they don't even get a dollar for it. Why are we changing everything in order to get another silly little trophy?"

The room was silent.

"But it means more than that, Claire," Charlotte said softly.

"It's one last chance for us to shine, and with our daughters by our side..."

"Not to me," Claire said.

Charlotte put her hand on her shoulder. "What's wrong, Claire?"

Claire began to cry. At first, large tear drops formed in the corners of her eyes, then they spilled over, trailing down her powdered checks. Her lips disappeared as she tried to hold on, as though she might explode, and then she couldn't hold on any longer.

"I've been stealing!" she cried out, falling prostrate across her calendar.

"What?" the others said in unison.

Claire's sobs echoed loudly inside her arms. "I've been using some of the money, ever since I went on Social Security," she sobbed. "None of you know this but it's impossible to survive on Social Security!"

How could they understand? They had no idea what it was like to live paycheck to paycheck. The business had been a lifesaver. At first, she had borrowed only a little here and there, but she always paid it back. And then, when there seemed to be so much extra, she started keeping a little more, and only because she had needed it so badly.

Claire's job was simple. She had been the Garden Club's treasurer for years so it made sense that she would handle the business. There was always more than enough to cover the Club's expenses. They had not had to charge for lunch in years and the road trips were completely covered by the Club.

"How much?" SueBee asked, gently rubbing her knuckles up and down between Claire's shoulder blades. "It can't be that much."

Claire sniffled and wiped her nose with a tissue Charlotte had handed her. "About one-fifty a week?"

"Is that all?" said Mona. "Heavens, Claire, that's a lunch at the country club. I don't mind that, do y'all?" No one did, but then Claire erupted again, scaring them all.

"I mean, no, it's more, I just can't say it," she sobbed.

Charlotte was now rubbing up and down her arm, trying to comfort her.

"Then exactly how much more?" SueBee asked.

"I only use about half..."

"How much?" Mona repeated. Claire held the tissue to her nose and looked around the table.

"We make about three thousand a month. I usually keep half to make ends meet."

Mona blurted out, "You mean fifteen hundred? A hundred fifty with an extra zero?"

Charlotte was genuinely surprised. "We make that much? Boy, if Gina knew that we'd be in big trouble."

Claire shook her head frantically. "Oh, please no. She has no idea and she can't know. If it got back to her office it would be terrible and she would probably never speak to me again. I'm a double criminal. A triple criminal." Claire buried her face in her hands again and sobbed. "I don't know what to do."

Mona drummed her nails on the table, and when Claire's sobs subsided, she said, "Claire, you don't need to worry. Gina isn't going to find out. This is just between us, alright? I'm glad it's finally out. Yes, it was wrong, but we are a family. You know that. You needed it." She waited for Claire to nod. "Then you should have told us."

"Now what are you going to do?" asked Charlotte.

"Don't worry about me, this is my problem," she said, wiping her nose with the tissue.

"Stop it, Claire. We have two things to solve together."

"What do you mean?" said Claire, her voice muffled behind her tissue.

"First of all, win or lose, we need to make sure our friends at The Village get what they need and second of all, how do *you* get what you need?"

Claire hiccupped a sob. She stretched out her hand toward Mona, who took it and squeezed it gently.

"You should have told us a long time ago," said Mona. "We would have understood." She leaned over and hugged her, then whispered something into the frizzy head. Finally she let her loose before resuming her usual demeanor.

"We're wasting time. I think our first meeting should be on containers."

"Wait a minute. I disagree," said SueBee. "I think we should do flower arranging first. How can they know what kind of container to use until they know about the construction?"

"I'll call the florist," said Charlotte. "We should have a program with the professionals."

"That's fine, but the first lesson will be this Wednesday on containers. That is the foundation for everything else. We'll meet here, at my house," said Mona. "I'll start the phone tree and Claire, please make sure the daughters know. And tell them not to be late."

CHAPTER 16

Gina couldn't sleep. Ever since she'd discovered the pot on Friday at Mona's, her nights had been filled with staring at the ceiling and replaying the part where the mothers raised their hands announcing they, too, were growing weed in a silver closet.

How could this be happening? How could they do this? It was like playing Life, the board game, and instead of drawing *Congratulations, you now have triplets, a boat and a mortgage,* she had drawn, *Congratulations! You thought you were going to have a career in law enforcement but instead you've learned your mother is dealing drugs.*

On Wednesday, Gina went through security and rode the elevator up to the fourth floor of the County Courts Building. Exhausted, she looked around the large room that had been her office for the last five years. It was a cavern of fluorescent lighting, metal desks and grey dividers that smelled of bleach in the mornings and body odor in the afternoons. Gina stopped and poured herself a cup of black coffee while thinking about her future.

A promotion would mean a move to the fifth floor, where the senior detectives had a break room with a decent coffee maker and a refrigerator where you could keep your lunch. A move upstairs would also mean no more black leather and fake tattoos.

Gina was ready. She'd been a detective for five long years and had earned the promotion. Her close rate was as good as anyone's and she felt confident about the test. The third leg of the three-legged stool, though, was her boss, Captain Grigsby, the one in the glass cage. Without his recommendation, the test score didn't matter.

Gina settled in at her desk and fished out a stained file from a bottom drawer. She flipped through the pages of the year-old case. There'd been six robberies in her old neighborhood and she still had nothing. Gina took another sip of the coffee, trying to wake up. She wanted this one badly.

Gina looked out her window. It was going to be a hot one and she noticed her arm closest to the window was already pink from the sun. She could see the blue outline of the Sheraton Hotel two blocks away. West of that was another hotel, Conrad Hilton's first, and at this time of day it magnified the brunt of the morning sun. The Aristocrat, she thought, or something like that.

On the other side of the Aristocrat was Neiman-Marcus's flagship store and on the second floor of Neiman's was the Zodiac Room, a restaurant where little girls had tea with grandmothers and bridal parties met for lunch. Gina pictured the piping hot popovers that were bigger than her hand. As a little girl, she had peeled back the corners to let the steam out, then dropped in a butter curl and watched it melt until she couldn't stand it anymore, eating the flaky layers.

Her eyes returned to the file. This case was the only thing she would hate leaving undone. Suddenly, with a loud snap, a white folder hit her desk. By the time she had looked up, Captain Grigsby was already on his way back to his office. He did that sometimes.

Gina heard a few snickers from the guys around her. She ignored them and picked up the file. "The Village" was written in the Captain's distinct scrawl. That was unusual. Files normally came from the on-duty desk officer. If this one came straight from the Captain, something was different. She opened it and started to read.

The notes were brief. Mr. Crawley, an administrator at The Village, had called to complain about drugs. Three phrases were underlined and circled. 'Suspicious,' 'Drugs?' and then '75-95.'

Gina glanced at Captain Grigsby in his glass office. She picked up the phone.

"Yeah?"

"Hey, Captain."

"What?" They stared at each other through the glass. Gina continued. "I'm looking at these notes on this file you just dropped on my desk, and..."

"You better not be calling me to complain, Sessions. Everyone's busy and this one shouldn't take long. It's a potential PR nightmare so investigate and solve it, like yesterday." It was hard to concentrate, hearing his voice through the phone while watching his lips move behind the glass.

"I'm not calling to complain, sir,but I have some questions about the notes."

"What," he asked, though it wasn't a question.

"What's The Village and what does '75-95' mean?"

"You got a computer, use it." There was a loud click as he hung up.

Gina rolled her eyes. She jiggled the mouse on her computer. Half way down the screen, the Dallas address for The Village popped up. She clicked on it. A single page opened up to a picture of a landscaped complex of high end apartments. "Enjoy Life! Come Live With Us!" was strung across the top of the page in bright red lettering. It was a moderately-priced retirement home and most of its residents were between the ages of seventy-five and ninety-five. The site listed Rusty Crawford as the Managing Director, and it also made a point of announcing that over fifty per cent of the residents were former residents of Hillcrest Heights.

Gina stared at the statistic, then picked up the phone and dialed. Her mother answered on the fifth ring.

"Mom?"

"Yes? Oh hi, honey, my phone was in the bottom of my purse. Where are you?" Gina could hear voices in the background.

"I'm at work."

"Are you on your way? I'm already at Mona's. If you get here soon she's still serving a light breakfast. You're coming, aren't you? We're going to talk about containers and you really need to hear this."

"I'll be there, Mom, but I need to ask you something." She cursed silently while resting her head in her hand, her eyes closed. She'd forgotten about the meeting at Mona's.

"What is the name of the place that the Garden Club has had the most, uh, *experience* with over the last several years?" Gina asked.

"What?"

Gina pressed her lips close to the receiver and whispered, "Where do you sell the marijuana?"

"It's the, the, oh, let me think. What is the name of that real nice place that overlooks the lake and I know at least some of the rooms have a view? Don't you remember, you took me to visit Miss

Sadie from church and they tried to sell me a room that looked straight into another building and said they were going to tear it down and then I'd have a view, but then Nita told me that they probably wouldn't tear it down for at least another five years..."

"Mom!"

"I think it's called The Village."

Gina covered the mouthpiece and looked around the room. No one seemed to notice.

"Why?" her mother asked.

"I'll tell you later."

"Well, hurry up and get over here, if you want to eat."

Gina hung up the phone and dialed a different number. The ring went to voice mail and Gina left a message.

"Hi, it's Gina. I need to meet. Page me when you get this."

The situation had suddenly gone from bad to worse. She and the other daughters had already decided that since winning the flower show was impossible, they needed a Plan B. They would do their best to learn everything the mothers wanted to teach them, but when they inevitably lost, the mothers would be so pleased with their dedication that they would finally agree that their daughters didn't need to start their own club to live happy fruitful lives. Even better, the mothers would agree that they were too old to be growing and selling marijuana. It might take a little longer, but the daughters thought it just might work.

But now, everything had changed. The Village was in the crosshairs of the department.

Gina raced the Jeep across town, up Young Street, past the Convention Center and City Hall, to a small side street past the farmers' market. Even though it meant being late, she had decided to stop by her condominium to change.

Her unit was twelve floors up in a converted office building that overlooked three major freeways. It was also in walking distance of the open market where farmers sold fresh fruits and vegetables under block-long arbors.

Gina parked in the underground garage, then rode up to the ground floor. Since it had originally been an office building the first floor was open and had a concierge and a florist shop that sold newspapers. Her footsteps echoed in the mostly tile and glass lobby. Gina spoke to the little man at the desk and boarded one of the elevators.

She'd been living in the Grayson Building for almost five years. Built in the '70s, the rent was reasonable and she liked the fact that it had real rooms, not just open spaces where there were no walls, except for the bathrooms. She never understood how people could accept living, eating, and sleeping in different corners of the same room. It just didn't make sense to her.

Natural light poured into Gina's living room from a wall of windows. There was a cozy arrangement of a couch and chairs in front of a small brick fireplace that she'd painted white. Stacks of books lay on a scarred and stained coffee table. The couch was covered in a knobby, soft grey material and there were dents in the cushions that showed where she'd been sitting. A delicate table with spindly legs displayed photos of Gina and her mother, her graduation from the police academy, and a picture of her father when he was a boy. A tall Chinese vase held some very nice plastic flowers.

As soon as she walked in, Bad Guy, her giant orange tabby, started meowing painfully, pawing at the balcony doors.

"I'm coming, I'm coming." Gina opened the doors and he padded quickly to his litter box. She look out over the street below where the noise was a constant throb.

Back inside, Gina stripped off her work clothes and put them in a paper sack. She changed into a simple blue dress, snipping off the tags then slipped into a pair of flats.

"See ya', boy. Got a command performance." The cat looked happy to see her go as she grabbed the paper bag and locked the door behind her.

Gina pressed the elevator button. She could hear the whine of the motor and cable, wheezing like an old man as it moved at a geriatric pace. She pressed the button again. Finally, the bell dinged and the doors slowly opened. She was about to step in when the door to the stairwell at the end of the hall opened and a man exited. He was breathing hard and checking his watch, as though he'd run up the twelve flights of stairs.

The first thing she saw were his long legs, then the sculptured muscles. His face was hidden inside a hoodie sweatshirt and just as she was about to step into the elevator, she took a last glance. At the exact same moment, he looked up and their eyes met. Gina saw that it was Blake.

Gina threw her foot into the door.

"Blake?"

"Gina? Hi."

"What are you doing here?"

"What am I doing here? What are you doing here?"

She nodded toward her door. "I live here."

"Really?" He nodded toward another door. "Me, too."

"You're the new tenant?"

"For the last four months."

The elevator alarm started to sound and she stepped off, then the doors started to close, until she pushed them open again, this time with her hand.

"You want to get lunch?" he asked. "I just need to take a quick shower."

The door kept fighting to close. She was swimming in his eyes, especially the one with the hairline scar over his brow.

"Sure, oh, wait, I can't. Another thing for my mom. I'm sorry, I've got to go, I'm late."

"Another one?"

"I know." The door chimed and she stepped inside but kept her hand on the doors. "I had a nice time the other day. What a coincidence," she said, lingering.

"Do you really have to go?"

She smiled as the doors closed between them.

CHAPTER 17

Claire couldn't help herself. Her eyes darted from the door to the clock over the microwave in Mona's kitchen and back again. There were at least thirty women, evenly split between mothers and daughters, helping themselves to coffee and a shrinking selection of pastries and fruit that had been set up in the breezeway. She hoped Gina would get there soon.

"Good morning," Mona announced from the far end of the kitchen. "It's a quarter past, so let's get started. SueBee, go ahead and start handing out those calendars. Everyone, you'll see we've planned several meetings over the next three weeks. I know it looks like a lot, but we have a lot to cover. Did everyone bring their Schedules?"

At the mention of the thick white manual, there was some uncomfortable shifting among the daughters but several manuals appeared. Claire couldn't help but think about the first time she'd leafed through page after page of do's and don'ts and technical jargon that no one understood.

"Once you start working with the flowers and doing your own arrangements, I think you'll be surprised how easy it is. And I know you can learn quickly because you have your mothers' genes. And surely you must have some talent of your own."

The kitchen door directly behind Mona slowly opened and Gina entered the room. She moved quickly to the back to stand next to Claire. The room waited for her.

"I'm glad you could join us, Gina," she said, glancing at her watch. "Fifteen minutes - I think that might be a record. As I was saying, the reading material and rules about containers are on pages 15 through 19 so be sure and read them later. Now, everyone, follow me over to this side of the kitchen." She stopped beneath an overhead row of cabinets. The members dutifully shifted.

"You look so pretty, Gina," Claire said under her breath. The dress brought out the blue in her eyes and there was something in her smile that Claire didn't quite know how to read.

"Sorry I'm late."

Mona began pulling out containers from the cabinets.

"Why don't you get something to eat?" Claire whispered, motioning with her cane toward the table of pastries and coffee.

Gina shook her head no before spotting a fruit tray. She inched over and filled a small bowl full of blueberries.

"There's something I need to tell you, Mom," Gina said, eating a handful of the fruit while Mona continued to lecture in the background.

Her mother waited.

"I got a new case this morning. The Village."

Claire gripped Gina's arm and maneuvered them both outside of the kitchen.

"Our Village?" she asked, her voice trembling.

"Yep," Gina said before popping in another handful of blueberries. "I probably shouldn't tell you, but then again, I thought you might want to pass that along." She motioned toward Mona. "We should probably go back in there."

"Who told? How in the world?"

"Who knows, The Village is a big place."

"What do you know about The Village?"

"I don't know, Mom. Maybe you could tell me."

"Gina!"

"Claire? Gina? Please, pay attention," Mona barked from the front before continuing. "...and please note, we will be having a *practice* flower show with judges, but more on that later..."

Gina lowered her voice. "The Garden Club needs to wrap things up, Mom. My boss has given me this new case and it doesn't look good. Investigations take time, but I have to work it and you know what that means. My boss is going to expect results so Garden Club needs to stop as soon as possible. Preferably now." Gina put the empty dish on the table and wiped her fingers on a napkin.

"I don't know," mumbled Claire.

"Mom, I just told you, we're starting an investigation. Please, stop. Get the others to stop."

"But I'm not the only one in charge," Claire said, staring straight ahead. Her mind was racing.

"I'll talk to them, but you know how stubborn they are," she said, avoiding Mona's glare from the other room. She started back toward the group. "Come on, you need to hear this. She's talking about containers."

A muffled buzzing noise sounded from Gina's purse. Mona looked visibly irritated as everyone watched Gina check a small black device before moving toward the door.

"Sorry," she apologized, holding up an old pager for all to see. "Work."

CHAPTER 18

From Mona's, Gina went east and south, past wealthy homes and manicured lawns, until she'd arrived in a part of Dallas where people lived with less of everything.

It was like a B-movie backdrop. There were dark and dingy storefronts. Fast food bags and cups floated in muck-filled gutters and graffiti-covered trash cans overflowed with garbage. Almost every corner was a trifecta—gas station, quick cash business, liquor store—which explained the shotgun homes with barred windows and doors.

Traffic was light and she'd made good time. Gina suddenly pulled right and parked where she could see a bus stop a few store fronts down. There were only a few people on the sidewalk and they didn't hide their curiosity. Gina's car and skin color didn't belong and she was glad she'd taken the time to change back into her work clothes before leaving Mona's.

Gina concentrated on the bus stop where a young man huddled into a corner of the bench. His head hung low and his hands were thrust deep into the pockets of his baggy jeans.

She checked the mirror and ran a finger under her eyes, then pulled her hair into a short, messy ponytail and rubbed off the pink lipstick. She found a pair of flip flops in the back and put them on, then got out of the car.

"Hey, Theo."

Theo was an eighteen year old black male, medium build, diamond stud earring in the left ear kid. Over the last five years she'd come to know a lot more about him. He was a sullen soul who preferred not to speak and he hardly ever smiled. Gina had always thought there was something innocent behind his eyes.

She'd first met Theo after a drug bust in south Dallas. She'd seen him lurking around the police cars and was just about to tell him to beat it when a horrible sound came from under the house. It almost sounded like someone was dying.

The old frame house sat on concrete blocks. During the day, if you squatted down low, you could see all the way across to the other side but in the dark there were only shadows.

There was a second howl and Gina shivered. Both of them knelt down and peered into the darkness. Whatever it was, it was alive. Bribed with a leftover cheese stick, the dog-size animal slowly crawled out from under the house and in the glare of her flashlight they realized it was actually a cat. It had greasy, matted fur and its tail had a cartoonish crook in it. One ear was torn, and both eyes were crusty, giving it a swarthy pirate look.

Gina had wrapped the cat in a blanket and heaved it like a barbell into the backseat of her car. The kid had watched sympathetically, then told her she was a typical white lady falling for a stupid cat. That's when she named him Bad Guy and brought him home.

"Bad Guy says hello," Gina told Theo.

"Right." He obviously wasn't there for small talk.

"I got two things I need you to do."

"What?"

"First, I need to know what you've heard about a crew working old folks' homes."

"Say wha?" he said, leaving off the t.

"Retirement homes, assisted living places. You know, where old people go. If you hear of anyone selling to them, I need to know."

Like most of their meetings, she was the only one talking and she could tell he was having trouble with this one.

"Just keep your ears open. Okay?"

He shrugged and shrunk back down. "Your money."

"Second, we're still working those home burglaries up north that I asked you about a few months ago." Theo knew 'up north' meant the Hillcrest Heights area.

"Remember, it's strictly designer junk like ladies' clothes, bags, jewelry. You sure you haven't heard of anyone trying to sell that kind of stuff?"

Theo shrugged and shook his head no.

Gina slid a twenty across the bench. Theo looked at it, but made no move to take it. She knew what he wanted and added another twenty. Theo took it in a smooth move, then stood from his slouch and walked to the edge of the curb as a city bus slowed to a stop in front of him. He turned and looked her in the eye. His mouth broke into a sideways grin. Gina smiled back at him, then watched him get on the bus and disappear down the street.

Back at the office, Gina had a hard time concentrating. She stared at her notes on The Village but her mind wandered back to Blake and the look on his face as the elevator doors closed. She smiled remembering the hopeful look in his eyes.

Her mind wandered to another meeting. It would be casual, accidental in fact, when they would both be waiting for the elevator. He would invite her to dinner. Maybe they would watch a little TV and then he would suggest she watch him paint, which she would. He would be amazing, and she would almost cry, having been so moved by his art. She would even lean into the painting, close enough to feel the heat from his body and he would feel hers. Knowing her, she'd become nervous and embarrassed and so she'd move away to the couch. But he would follow her, after struggling to choose between his painting and her. Then he'd come and sit down close to her, knowing she was waiting for him.

Then what would she do? Gina had to think.

Oh yes, she would offer to rub his back. First she would massage his hands, those long rough hands with the pale clipped nails and paint stuck in the cuticles. She'd rub his arm and then his shoulders, his back, touching him...

"Oooh," Gina said, shaking her head to clear it. She could feel her heart racing and looked around to make sure no one noticed. She took a deep breath. "Lord, help me," and took a long drink of a water bottle, wishing she could splash a little on her face.

It was after five when she arrived back at her condo. Gina stepped off the elevator and immediately looked toward Blake's door. The hallway felt like a tomb. It was quiet and empty except for the background music piped through the vents. She began walking very, very slowly toward her door, humming a little louder than usual, then whistling. Outside her door, she dug in her purse, found her keys, letting them fall to the floor. While on her knees, she looked at Blake's door, then Bad Guy meowed pitifully from the other side of her own.

"Oh, shut up, Bad Guy," Gina said, putting her key in the door.

The elevator dinged. Gina's hand froze and while the cat whined loudly, as the metal doors opened and her next door neighbor, Mrs. Stein, stepped off the elevator carrying two webbed sacks of groceries.

"Good evening, Gina." She had a thick German accent and wore a small brown hat to cover her head, a few silver wisps of hair escaping. She set down the bags in front of her door.

"Good evening, Mrs. Stein. Let me help you with your bags."

"No, no, I'm almost there." She set them down and began fishing out a string from between her breasts. "I never see you, dear, and yet there you are, dressed in black again. Another funeral?"

"Yes, ma'am, and how are you doing?"

By now the string was at least two feet long, almost half of Mrs. Stein's height. Finally she got to the end and put the key in the door.

"Actually, Gina, I'm glad to see you. I'd like to invite you to come to dinner tonight. I know this is late, so rude, but my grandson is coming and I'm making a very nice borscht. Would you like to join us?"

Gina didn't have to think long, picturing the four-foot-tall relative. "That's so kind of you, Mrs. Stein, but I have so much to do tonight and it's been a long day." On cue Bad Guy let out another, more pitiful howl. "My cat."

"Oh well, I understand," she said, waving a boney hand, "but I shouldn't ask. That is also rude of me."

"Oh no, thank you. Another time maybe?" The tortured sounds continued and Gina pointed toward her door. "But thank you, Mrs. Stein. I better get in there."

Mrs. Stein shrugged her understanding, then disappeared behind the wreath.

Gina opened the door to the empty apartment and followed Bad Guy to his bowl. She ate cheese and crackers for dinner, cleaned up a little, then stood at the open doors to her balcony where she could hear music coming from Mrs. Stein's over the dull roar of the freeways below. A warm breeze blew against her face as strains of violin music floated from the open windows next door.

Gina's neighbor didn't have a balcony, only windows that spanned the width of her unit, but they were open and even though they were separated by a thick brick wall, she could hear the music quite clearly. Stepping to the edge of her patio, she stood, listening to the music. Usually the wind and noise from the street below gave everyone a sense of privacy. But tonight it must have been blowing in a different direction because if she leaned just a little further toward her neighbor's windows, she could actually hear them laughing.

Gina edged closer and by holding on to her own railing, she was able to stretch just far enough over the brick until she could actually see into the old lady's living room. The violin music got louder. Tall plants blocked her view so she had to stretch even further but then she could see that the dining room was lit by the warm glow of lamplight.

Mrs. Stein's back was to the window, her guest seated across from her. Carefully, Gina gripped the edge of the brick wall that separated their units and with her feet hooked around the rungs of her balcony, she was able to lean forward and move one inch closer. Suddenly, Mrs. Stein's guest stood up.

Gina swung herself backward against her own wall. Her heart beat wildly in her chest. She held her breath and heard a man's voice.

"I don't know, I thought I saw something."

Gina's heart stopped. She recognized Blake's voice.

"Hello?" he called into the darkness. They were twelve floors up and Gina breathed a prayer.

"I know you're over there, Gina."

She cursed the air. "Hi."

"Are you stalking me?"

Gina was shocked. "What?"

"You show up at my apartment, my grandmother's, Jackson's. I'm starting to think I may need to file a complaint."

"That is ridiculous. This is my apartment. And Jackson's is mine. I can't believe..." and then Gina stopped, realizing he was laughing at her.

"Very funny. You could have told me your grandmother was my next door neighbor."

"I guess I could have. But this is a lot more fun."

"Blake? Who's out there?" Mrs. Stein's voice came from inside.

"It's Gina, Grandmother."

"Ask her to come for soup."

"Did you hear that?"

"Thanks, Mrs. Stein. Maybe another time."

Blake's voice was suddenly quiet. "How about breakfast, next Saturday?"

Gina screwed up her face, hating her answer. "You aren't going to believe this, but…"

"Your mom?" Blake finished for her.

"It's only for a couple more weeks. I'm helping her with this important thing. But I'd like to, just another time."

"Shake on it?" he asked.

Gina reached her hand as far as she could across the wall that divided them and waved it in space. In a second, she felt his strong fingers envelope hers.

CHAPTER 19

Gina held the mug of black coffee to her lips as she replayed the feel of Blake's fingers gripping hers. Butterflies took off in her stomach and she smiled in a semi-dream state until a drunk fell out of his chair one cubicle over.

A cool breeze from the open window next to her desk brushed her cheek. Normally, she hated the paper thin glass and chipped wood frames because they sweated in the winter and got stuck in the summers. But today, she'd fought them open to their full height and was overwhelmed with the peaceful pleasure of filling her lungs with sunshine. Even the back and forth sounds of overweight buses gunning from their scheduled stops did nothing to spoil the moment.

Gina sighed and put down the cup and thought about the warning she'd gotten that morning on her answering machine.

1:00, her mother's house, don't be late, and be prepared to do your own arrangement. Gina cringed. They weren't going to be watching someone else make an arrangement. Not anymore. Now they were going to be all on their own. Gina had searched all morning, making her late to work, for the perfect container. She'd looked through every cabinet and finally found an old glass vase over the washing machine, tangled in a pile of extension cords. It was a drab shade of green. Everyone else's would probably be perfect.

Gina withdrew the heavy Schedule from a bottom drawer and turned to a section that she'd bookmarked with a glossy page from *Homes and Gardens*. She studied the picture of a flower arrangement, then compared it to a list of do's and don'ts on the opposite page. A pencil held between her lips jiggled as she judged how best to copy it for the practice flower show.

"What are you doing, Sessions?" Captain Grigsby asked, dropping into the empty chair by her desk.

Gina nearly bit through the pencil as she jerked forward and draped her arms over the Schedule.

"What's up?" The pencil dropped out of her mouth.

"That's what I want to know. What's going on with the old folks thing?"

"The Village? Oh, it's going fine."

"And?"

"Well," she began slowly, "I've made a few calls. And I talked with my informant. I'm sure he'll come up with something. This is a tough one, Captain. Old people are frail, you know."

"Right," he said, but he obviously didn't agree. "So what did you find out when you went over there?"

"Well, I haven't been yet, like I said..." She stopped. His eyes had been scanning the office like a mother bird looking for prey, but now they were focused on her. Gina shifted uncomfortably in her seat.

"Don't take this one slow, Sessions. I told you to go after it because I'm getting pressure from the mayor's office. Get over there. I thought you'd like an easy one, especially since you want that promotion so bad, but if you don't, I got plenty of others who would. I just thought since you had the last drug bust..."

"Actually, I'm just about to go over there," she interrupted.

"What a coincidence." He looked curiously at the file underneath her arms. "Anything new on the burglaries?"

She shook her head no.

"Somehow I knew you were going to say that. They're keeping score upstairs, Sessions. You know that, right? I'd hate to see you blow it."

"I won't blow it."

"Pick up the pace, Sessions, with the robberies and The Village." He wrapped his knuckles on her desk like a period and got up to leave.

"I'll be sure and threaten Grandma with an Indian burn," she said to his back.

The Captain slowly turned. A cold expression had come over his face and she felt the hairs on her arms stand up.

"If you happen to pass that test, it doesn't mean the promotion is yours. You need a recommendation from my desk, okay? You want that, you get this done." He studied her again. "Maybe you ought to think about wearing a dress when you go see those old folks. Old men can't resist a pretty lady."

Gina made sure he was back in his glass-enclosed office before dropping deeper into her chair, and began picking out shredded pieces of pencil that were still in her mouth.

An hour later, she arrived at The Village Retirement Home and followed the signs to visitor parking. She passed a vacant security booth and saw four two-story buildings around a central park-like setting. Large trees provided plenty of shade for residents as they were being helped along the winding paths in wheelchairs and walkers. Some had aides, others walked alone.

She parked, then walked around, noting entrances and exits. She tried a couple of doors. Both opened. Gina passed several employees, none of whom questioned who she was. Finally, inside, a receptionist pointed Gina toward the administrator's office where Mr. Crawley got right to the point.

"I've worked here for almost six months now, got transferred from New York because my wife wants to live where it's warm, see, and now here we are, right in the middle of the Bible belt, and I think there's something fishy going on."

"Like what?" Gina asked, opening a small notebook.

"I've worked with senior citizens for thirty years and..." He stopped, as if he was almost too amazed himself to continue, then leaned forward in his chair and put both hands on his desk. "I'd thought I'd seen it all but I've never seen this." Gina waited while Mr. Crawley took a big breath and shook his head side to side before continuing. He seemed to be enjoying the drama.

"Usually, and I'm bein' honest wid ya' here, these places are depressing. The way it's supposed to go is the staff and me, it's our job to keep things cheerful, ya know? Lively. We offer bingo, singalongs, quiet things like that. And normally, well, mediocre happy is about all we get because most of them have decided they've come here to die. They're not on vacation. You know what I mean?"

She nodded.

"So, I get here, and right away, they tell me they don't want to do singalongs, they don't care about playing a quiet game of bingo, and they don't want to learn how to paint. They want..." He paused, searching for the right word. "They tell me they like *action*. They're used to playing poker, with *real* money, and they want swing dancing and R-rated movies. I even have to make sure the nurses keep track of one guy who thinks he's a regular Romeo or something. 'We're all adults, here,' they keep saying. And do you know what the weird part is? Hardly anyone complains. That's not normal, Officer. I even had to let one of our doctors go because no one ever called. They're just so darn cheery."

"Isn't that a good thing?"

"It's not normal! Somethin' is definitely, and I mean def-i-nit-ly up with these people. And then, bingo! One of the nurses finds this marijuana cigarette in Mr. Jones' waste basket. 'That's it,' I say to myself. It's drugs! I'm from New York, lady, and I shoulda' seen it comin' a mile away. They're happy 'cause they're high. And if you want to know what else I think, I think Mr. Jones is the ringleader. He's real smart and even though he can't get around, he always knows what's going on with everybody. That's the guy I'm watchin' but so far, I haven't found anything else. But now you're here and you've got to stop it.

Gina stopped taking notes. "Do you still have the cigarette?"

He reached into a drawer and proudly handed her the butt. She smelled it and nodded.

"Maybe it belonged to a visitor?"

"Mr. Jones doesn't get visitors."

"Maybe staff?"

"Sure, it could be staff. But if you knew how tough it was to get a job in one of these places, I'd say it's highly unlikely. They get tested all the time and they know if they do anything like that, they're gone. No severance, nothin'. And this is the best facility in town. I really don't think they'd risk it. And like I'm trying to tell you, I knew something was wrong the first week I was here."

Gina stared at her notes.

"Well?"

She thought a moment longer. "So you think the patients are getting marijuana from somewhere?"

"Didn't I just say that? Now it's your job to figure out how. I'm probably going to lose mine, not to mention 136 lawsuits."

Gina did feel a little sorry for the man. She tried to look serious and made a few more notes in her book.

"Let me ask you a few questions, Mr. Crawley. I noticed there's a security booth at the entrance to the property but no one was in there. Is that normal?"

"It's a budget thing. I've never been able to afford a full-time guard. Everyone's supposed to check in with the receptionist, like you did, but with family members coming and going all day, sometimes in the night, we rely on the staff to ask questions if they don't recognize someone."

"I hate to tell you this, but they don't. I walked all around this place and not one person questioned me. And most of the doors are wide open."

"But we've never had a problem."

"Except for the drugs."

"Yeah, I guess you could say that."

The manager wrung his hands. "So what are you going to do?"

"I'm going to try and help you, Mr. Crawley, but it's going to take some time," Gina put the book in her back pocket. "I'll need a list of residents and employees, and if you've got a layout of the buildings that would be helpful. I want to be very careful in how I go about this investigation. I don't want to scare someone if they aren't involved and if they are guilty, I need to figure out the best way to confront them. I'm sure it's only a few trouble makers we're talking about." She got up to leave.

"Mr. Crawley, I'm just curious. Are there any high profile residents here?"

He answered right away. "I guess you might consider the mayor's mother high profile. He comes by every so often, always has an entourage with him. We try to make sure she's well taken care of and I think she's seems to be very happy here." Mr. Crawley suddenly frowned. "So how long do you think this will take?"

Gina pictured the calendar her mother had handed her at the last meeting. "Oh, I think it will take about three weeks," she said. "I can almost guarantee it."

CHAPTER 20

It was a nice surprise when Charlotte arrived early to help Claire set up the Club's folding tables for the Monday meeting with the daughters. It took some serious digging but they finally found the old metal tables packed against one of the walls in her garage. They were wedged in between Christmas wreaths and headboards and were covered in dust and spider sacs.

"Claire?" called a high-pitched voice.

"We're in here, Henry," Claire answered back. A short man in a salmon golf shirt rounded the corner, his arms full of floral supplies.

"We'll have your table cleaned off in just a minute," said Claire. She took a clean towel and wiped but it still looked filthy. "Should I get you a tablecloth?"

"No, no, no. Time to get dirty, that's my motto." He turned on his toes and headed back to the van for more supplies. The tables were soon cluttered with sacks and buckets. Charlotte and Claire laid things out so that each daughter would have flowers, tape, a towel, clippers, and gloves.

Just before one, the daughters straggled in. Gina was only a little late when Mona called the room to order. She stood in front of a tall vase, a bucket of flowers, and some clippers.

"I'm here to help, but only if you need it," Claire whispered in Gina's ear. She'd moved quickly to stand behind her. The other mothers had done the same behind their daughters.

"Before I let Henry get started," began Mona loudly, "I have an important announcement. We've decided to move your practice flower show up to this coming weekend so please, add that to your calendars. After that you'll have two full weeks to get ready for the big show."

"This weekend?!" Gina blurted out.

"Do you really think we're ready?" asked Sheralyn.

"Of course not," laughed Mona. "The whole purpose is to help you see your weaknesses."

Sheralyn whimpered.

"But that's how you learn," volunteered Charlotte. "And you know we don't expect perfection."

"Ha," said Gina.

"Gina," insisted Claire from behind, "please! It really is for your benefit. Seeing the judges' comments will help you."

"Oh, that makes me feel so much better."

"Alright everyone, pay attention," said Mona. "Henry is going to show you how it's done. Enjoy!"

Henry had been quietly organizing his tools as though preparing for battle. Cutting utensils, picks, green tape and several containers of water were in front of him. There were also mounds of flowers of varying heights. The tallest was a stack of iris, a slightly smaller one of roses and another of peonies. There were also a few star gazers and then a wild and overflowing spot for the spiraea.

At Mona's announcement, he moved to the center of the table to stand in front of a tall wide vase. Reverently, Henry reached for a pink peony. He held it out for all to see, then rested the clippers about three inches from the base of the stem. The room was silent. Suddenly, he snapped the blades of the clippers and cut. There was a collective gasp.

"I've chosen three peonies to anchor my arrangement," he said without pausing. He picked up another peony and clipped decisively before thrusting it into the vase. He attacked a third, then a fourth and a fifth, all without taking a breath. The daughters watched, frozen at their tables, as though they were observing an execution.

"Wait!" said Brooke. "Please! How do you know where to cut?" She was holding her clippers in one hand and an iris in the other.

Henry raised a plucked brow.

"Just eyeball it and be brave. This is not an exact science and you can hardly ruin a beautiful flower. Trust me." He was now removing the tiniest of stems from a handful of the spiraea, then sliding it in among the larger flowers. Brooke looked like she was about to cry.

Claire watched Gina from behind. Her hand floated over several strong yellow irises. She was just about to make a suggestion when finally, Gina chose one. She measured the stem against the vase, then opened the mouth of the clippers, touched the flower to the blades, and hovered.

"For Heaven's sake, Gina, just start cutting," Claire urged from behind.

"I've got this, Mom." Gina adjusted herself more squarely to block her mother and moved the clippers up the stem. She made a motion to cut.

"Wait!"

"What?"

"Shouldn't you go a little lower?"

"I don't know, should I?" Gina moved her clippers to a slightly lower spot.

"Wait!"

But her mother was too late. Gina cut the flower and dropped it into the vase.

"How's that?" she asked.

"Can I please make a *tiny* suggestion?"

"No."

"If you'd start with your largest flower and make it the tallest one in the center, and then choose two more..."

"I've got this, Mom."

Claire hesitated, then picked up an extra pair of clippers.

"Here, I'll show you," she said, coming from behind.

"Oh heavens, Sheralyn, you're not drawing blood!" Mona's voice echoed from the other end of the table having already pushed Sheralyn aside.

By now, almost all the mothers were in front of their daughters. Their movements were quick and sure and when they were done, they ushered the girls back into place as though this were all perfectly normal.

"Wonderful, girls, wonderful," announced Henry, walking along the tables. He fingered a flower here and there and commented on a few that stood out. Claire held her breath. She could feel the tension coming off of Gina like a heat wave. Henry stopped in front of them.

"This is very nice, Gina. Very nice."

Claire closed her eyes and braced herself for whatever kind of comment Gina would make. But all she heard was a quiet, "thank you," and then Henry had moved on to the next arrangement. Claire let out her breath. Relief washed over her. It wasn't often that Gina held her tongue.

"Alright, ladies," Henry announced, "I think we have enough flowers for one more arrangement. Find a second container and let's see what you can do. And mothers, let's see what the girls can do on their own, shall we?"

After the meeting, the mothers stood at the end of the driveway and watched as each daughter carried two arrangements to their cars.

"We're never going to win," said Mona quietly from behind her dark glasses while the others shaded their eyes against the sun.

"I think Brooke did alright," said Charlotte. "She just needs some more practice." The daughters were talking at the end of the driveway under the shade of an old pecan tree.

Charlotte waved, calling, "See you Saturday! Bright and early! Don't be late."

"Helen had an interesting method," said SueBee. "It was like watching her diaper a baby. She held it down with one hand and managed everything else with the other."

"Gina acted like she was in a steer roping contest," said Claire. "I think she finished in five seconds flat."

"I have absolutely no hope in Sheralyn," said Mona. "I think we either need to meet every day or plan on doing more of the arrangements ourselves, which in that case, I don't think they deserve the silver."

"Mona! Listen to yourself. We don't need the silver any longer. If they do their best, they should have it."

"That's exactly my point. They seem so casual about it. This is a serious competition and they should be eating and sleeping flower arranging. Sheralyn hasn't asked me for any extra help. Have your girls?"

The others shook their heads no.

"They need to train, train, train. I don't think they really care."

"I don't believe that," said Charlotte. "I think they do. They're just are so busy."

"Stop making excuses for them," said Mona. "Don't forget, we have our reputations on the line."

Claire kept her mouth shut. Sometimes Mona could be so unlikeable but reminding her about prison wouldn't help.

"Oh look! They're waving!" said Charlotte.

"You are being too hard on them, Mona," said Suebee, "and for heaven's sake, they just started. This is new to them. They're going to get better every time. And remember, the practice show is going to be a big help. With judges and all. "

Mona shrugged. She obviously didn't think so.

"I'm going to call Brooke and see if she can get together to practice. Maybe we should all try that," suggested Charlotte.

"I don't know if that will work for us. Gina works, you know."

"Everyone knows Gina works, Claire. But everyone's busy. You must tell her she has to make the time," said Mona.

"I've given up trying to tell Gina what to do. It doesn't do any good."

"Don't worry," said SueBee, giving her a quick hug. "Just give it a try. You can lead a horse to water but you can't make her drink, and maybe, when this is all over, they'll decide they like each other enough to keep doing things together. It doesn't have to be a garden club."

"I doubt it. And by the way, since we probably aren't going to win, I still like Claire's idea to move everything."

"I wasn't being serious," said Claire.

"I still like it and I don't see why we can't figure something out," said Mona.

"The problem isn't where we keep it, the problem is getting caught because Gina has to do her job."

"Then we don't tell Gina and just do it."

Claire growled and threw her hands in the air. The others remained silent.

"Oh, look at the time," said Charlotte. "Shall we clean up?"

As one, they stepped back into the cool shade of the garage and silently worked in their efficient ways. Within minutes, things were packed away and the floor cleanly swept. The tension was gone as well.

They were all about to leave when Mona remembered something.

"Charlotte, do you want to go with me to The Village this afternoon? Jonas had to go to Tyler this week and asked if I could deliver things myself."

"Oh sure," said Charlotte, "if I can stop at the market on the way home."

Claire closed the garage door after them. She had a feeling that no matter what happened at the flower show, Gina was not going to be happy.

CHAPTER 21

Gina stood with the others at the end of the driveway beneath her mother's huge pecan tree that for now was shading Sheralyn's BMW. She was still holding her two arrangements like party favors.

"Well, that was a waste of time," she said.

"It wasn't that bad," said Brooke.

"It was a joke," said Gina. "And if we don't win, it's going to be a fight to the death to get them to stop growing weed."

"We have to win and I definitely need the practice," Helen said, "but without anyone looking over my shoulder."

"The actual doing it is really hard," Sheralyn admitted. "Every cut is so permanent."

Gina had watched how she'd wilted under Mona's eye. Everyone knew the old woman could not abide weakness and in Mona's eyes, Sheralyn's softness and sincerity translated into weakness.

"I'm going to go buy a ton of flowers and try doing whatever it was that Henry was doing," Sheralyn continued, wrapping strands of blond hair around her ears. "I have to figure this out or Mona's going to kill me."

"Does anyone else think this whole flower show thing might just be part of their plan?" said Brooke.

"I thought the plan was they need us to help them win the Excelsior," said Sheralyn.

Gina had moved to rest against the car. "What do you mean, Brooke?"

"What if they never thought we could win the Excelsior because that's not what they really care about. What they really want is to get us to do something together so that we'll change our minds about garden club. You know, come to our senses and realize we've always wanted to have a club like theirs. Look at them. They're probably hoping we're bonding right now."

The half circle of mothers stood at the other end of the driveway. Brooke waved and immediately, they all waved back.

"Wow," said Helen. "Either that or they're high."

Gina's mind raced. "Actually, Brooke, you could be right. And I think we just solved the problem of what happens if we don't win the Excelsior."

"What?" the others said in unison.

"We give them what they really want. Let's bond. We'll show them we want to learn their traditions and we'll try really hard to win the Excelsior, but even if we don't win, which is highly likely, it won't matter because they'll be so overjoyed we're carrying on their traditions, they'll do whatever we want."

"And then we start our own club?" asked Sheralyn.

"Are you kidding?"Gina checked her watch. She'd wasted enough of the day and needed to get back to work.

"So, everybody, let's be *enthusiastic*. Study your Schedules!" she said vigorously.

"I can do that," said Helen, starting for her minivan. "Listen, I'll see everybody. Car pool."

"Wait," said Sheralyn. She put out her hand into the center of their circle, palm down and looked expectantly at the others. One by one, they followed.

Gina put her hand on top.

"To the daughters," said Sheralyn.

"To the daughters!"

CHAPTER 22

Thursday morning, right after breakfast, Claire put on her straw hat and went outside to the backyard shed to get her red scooter. The life-sized structure was harvest gold and gave her sixty four square feet of storage. It sat at the far corner of her concrete patio and had a sloped roof so that birds could nest under its eaves. A single hook held the warped door closed.

Claire loved her shed. It's where she kept her battle-scarred shovels, clay pots, tomato plant cones and sheet metal chicken feeders, almost all of which she didn't use anymore but loved too much to give away. The scooter was about half her age and it barely had any paint left on its metal body. And even though the wheels were bent and rusted and the seat had lost its plastic cushion, like most old things, it still had a purpose.

Once she got it out of the shed, she tied a rope onto the handle and led it to the front yard where she was working when the sound of a car door made her turn.

"That's a handsome car," Claire said, looking past Gina at a shiny black Mercedes. "It's about time they let you drive something nice." She also noticed Gina's nice suit. Navy slacks with a matching jacket and tiny gold earrings.

Gina dropped down into the grass next to her.

"Why don't they ever let you drive a real police car?"

"If I drove a black and white it would sort of give things away. What are you doing? Don't you think it's too hot to be outside?"

"It's not that bad. Anyway, I'm almost done." Claire wiped away drops of sweat with the back of a gloved hand. She was feeling warm but needed to finish what she'd started. She'd been pulling hard at a tangle of lantana and had just given the roots a few karate chops with her trowel. She tossed a dismembered vine to a naked place further back in the bed.

"You look so nice today. Any reason?" She waited, hoping Gina would tell her about that man who'd picked her up but Gina didn't take the bait.

"Thank you. No reason."

"Anything new on your test scores?"

"Not yet. Maybe another week, but it could be after that."

"Why is it taking so long? I think Mona knows someone at City Hall. Do you want me to ask?"

"Definitely not."

"It wouldn't hurt."

"Please, Mom. It's alright. I don't mind waiting."

"I don't know why, but alright, if you don't want me to... Are you ready for Saturday? Where are you getting your flowers?"

"I don't know," Gina said absentmindedly, staring into the flower bed. She suddenly straightened. "I stopped by to see if you wanted to work together on an arrangement. Tonight maybe?"

Claire stopped digging. "You haven't ordered your flowers yet?"

"I'll pick some up after work," Gina said, picking at blades of grass again. "I'm asking if you want to work together tonight."

Claire couldn't stop herself. "You should have ordered your flowers at least on Monday. You don't just pick up flowers for a flower show the day you need them. They might not have what you want. You can't find decent flowers after five."

"Don't worry, Mom. I'll find some."

"But they won't be pretty." Claire hit the stool with the trowel.

"Do you want to get together tonight or not?"

Claire shook her head in disbelief. "Fine," Claire said, "but they aren't going to be pretty. What time?"

"Come about seven."

Claire felt the familiar tension in the air and tried to avoid it by turning back to her beds.

"Mom, have you ever wished your life had been different?"

The question seemed to come out of nowhere. "What?"

"You know, the Garden Club. Has it been hard being part of that life? They have so much, you have so little."

"Not really," she answered tentatively. "We have a lot more in common than that."

"But haven't you ever felt like you were an outsider?"

Claire looked back at the top of Gina's head.

"Stop pulling out my grass. I'm going to have a bald spot in my yard. I don't think I've ever felt that way."

Gina looked up. "Really?"

Claire shrugged her answer.

"I guess it's just me, then. I'm the only one that's not married, I don't have kids, I work, I'm a cop."

"Then why don't you ask them to include you in some of the things they do? I know Brooke is involved in the Symphony League."

"That's not the point, Mom. I'm not looking for things to do. I'm just saying we're very different."

"Oh. Well, I guess you are, but not in a bad way. I'm sure they love you the way you are."

"Really? Then why do I feel like you keep trying to help me be like them."

"I do not. Just because I want to help you, that's what mothers do. We want our children to be happy."

"No, you want me to be like them."

"Gina, I do not."

They stared at each other. Seconds passed.

Gina suddenly began dusting her hands of the grass and rose to her feet. "Fine. I need to go."

"Gina, wait. I don't mean to make you feel that way and I'm sorry if I do. But I will always try to help. That's just the way I am. I'm not sure you know what you're missing." Gina shrugged. "Now be honest, do you have doubts about yourself?"

"What does that mean?"

"I know your father wasn't around when you were a teenager, but he loved you very much. The only reason he left was because he felt responsible for losing everything. He was embarrassed, and ashamed. He thought things would be better for us without him but it had nothing to do with loving you less. I think I may have not done a very good job of teaching you that. Do you think you might have trouble trusting men?"

Gina laughed. "I'm not a lesbian, Mom. And I'm not repressed. Everything's okay. Please stop trying to figure me out, my God!"

"See? You're angry! And I think it might have something to do with what you think about men, and if you want to talk to someone..."

"I don't have a problem with men."

Claire mumbled quickly, "I didn't say you had a problem. I just want you to be happy."

"I am happy!" Gina yelled, stomping a foot.

"He always said he would rather you be angry at him than ashamed of him."

"Well, it worked. I'm now angry."

"Well, don't be angry at your father. The divorce was partly my fault, you know. It's never just one person and I don't know if I ever told you but I was the one in charge of keeping the books. I don't know why people keep putting me in charge of money but he did and I made some mistakes, but still, I don't want it to sound worse than it was. And then we lost everything and had a few legal problems."

"Did you break the law?"

"Not on purpose," Claire said, starting to feel better until Gina began waving her arms and walking in circles.

"This is like the Twilight Zone. Why can't you just play bridge? You're selling drugs and you want me to feel sorry for Dad? Who are you people?"

"Oh, Gina, stop being so dramatic! Your Dad knew you would be okay."

"I'm leaving. I need to go find someone to arrest," Gina said, turning to go.

"Wait," Claire called after her. She thought Gina might stop but she didn't. "You asked me if I felt different," she yelled across the yard, not caring if the neighbors were listening.

"I don't care, Mother," Gina sang back.

"You really should start your own club."

Gina whirled around. "Ah hah! Now the cat's out of the bag. That's the whole reason for this flower show, isn't it? But you know what? I am not even going to pretend it's a possibility. I'm happy! I don't need to be in a garden club. I don't care about the silver. I don't need to fit in! So when we don't win this trophy, I'm coming after the silver closets. And you can tell Mona I don't care who she knows at City Hall, she's going down."

Gina opened her car door and yelled, "I'm happy!"

"But it's never been about the flower arranging or the silver," Claire said, "it's always been about the people." But she was too late. Even if Gina had heard her, she wasn't listening.

The driver's window rolled down. "Never mind about practicing tonight, I'll see you Saturday. And please do not call me at six-thirty in the morning. I won't be late!"

CHAPTER 23

Gina was so busy at work on Friday she'd completely forgotten about the practice show until the sun began to set.

She finally got away from work and zigzagged through downtown, speeding to the nearest florist where she discovered they closed at six. She visited two more and both were also closed. As a last resort, Gina pulled into one of the big box stores and hoped they had what she needed.

Gina directed her cart past leftover Easter baskets and yard signs until she spotted a short end cap of gardening supplies. She threw several small bags of picks, some oasis, some heavy green foam, wire, and floral tape into the basket, then remembered seeing a refrigerated case near the front of the store. The flowers were dreadful and each sad-looking carnation and brown-edged rose seemed to embody her mother's words from Thursday. A sign stuck to the inside of the glass said, "Half off after five." Gina bought them all.

She was in no hurry to get home. With the supplies in the back, she drove aimlessly along familiar streets in the general direction of downtown. She hit a familiar speed bump a little too fast and the Jeep rattled but she didn't care. She couldn't wait for this whole flower show thing to be over.

As she drove through Hillcrest Heights, Gina glanced up an alley, then hit her brakes. Peering into the darkness, she watched as a pair of taillights flashed on, then off, then on again. It was as if someone were driving very slowly, but stopping and starting.

Gina froze. The hair on her arms stood up, her heart beat faster. She slowly let off the brake and let her car coast into the alley. Her hand touched the gun tucked inside her jacket then she cursed herself for leaving her vest in the trunk. She squinted again into the darkness where she could barely make out the outline of a late model minivan. An interior light went on and she could see the shape of the driver and a smaller person moving around inside. The light went off but it was definitely a minivan.

Gina allowed the Jeep to creep closer. At twenty feet away, she braked, turned on her headlights and the overhead police lights, and bolted from the car.

"Put your hands on the steering wheel," she commanded in a loud voice, pointing her flashlight at the driver's face. A woman's hands immediately clasped the wheel. Gina stepped closer.

"Helen?" Gina leaned down. Her friend was wearing oversized glasses and pajamas. She recognized Helen's youngest son Benji in the passenger seat looking giddy. He was also in pajamas.

"Gina," Helen said. "Hi! Benji look, it's Mommy's friend. Gina's mommy is in Garden Club with Granny."

"Hi," the little boy said brightly. There was a tiny space where a tooth had been in his smile and he thrust a handful of iris at her. Gina lowered her voice.

"What's going on, Helen?"

"I messed up my first batch of flowers practicing for the show tomorrow and I don't have time to get to the store but I knew there were plenty of flowers in the alley. We just live over there," she said, pointing.

"I know, but..."

"I'm helping," said Benji, holding out the iris again as proof.

"Benji, hurry up and put those in the bucket before they wilt." Like a gymnast, Benji rolled over the seat and into the back.

"How much do you have back there?"

"It's okay, Gina, we aren't going in anybody's yards, are we, Benji?" Helen looked in the rear view mirror at her son.

"No, ma'am," he shouted from the back. "I just reach out and pull 'em through the fence."

Gina took a harder look inside the van. Buckets of freshly cut flowers filled the rear cargo space.

"No one's going to miss a few flowers," said Helen. She looked in the mirror again, "but don't tell Daddy, just in case."

Benji nodded enthusiastically.

"Maybe not, but if the neighbors knew you were sneaking in their alley, I don't think they'd like it. What if someone actually called the police?"

"Oh, I don't think they'd do that. But that's okay. I think we have enough. How is your arrangement coming?"

"I haven't even started," said Gina, but didn't elaborate.

"Well, good luck." Helen put the van in gear. "Mom and I have been practicing all week – so she definitely thinks I'm gung ho on the garden club thing. But it's so much harder than I thought. Would you like some of mine? I have plenty."

"I'm good, but thanks," said Gina.

"Well, alrightee then." The van began pulling forward. "Thank you, Officer. Isn't this exciting, Benji? Mommy's friend is a policeman."

Gina stepped back as they pulled away, but then the van stopped and Helen leaned out her window. "Are you sure you don't want some? I have so many."

"Goodnight, Helen."

Gina's arms were loaded with crackling cellophane-wrapped flowers as she rode up the elevator to the twelfth floor. She found some plastic buckets and filled them with water, then trimmed the stems as she'd been shown by Henry before putting them in the cold water. Then she spread her newly purchased supplies across the kitchen counter like a surgeon preparing for surgery.

"Plenty of time to throw this baby together. Right, Bad Guy?" The cat stared hungrily at the flowers from across the room, his crooked tail flicking hypnotically.

"Forget it, cat. I'm not letting you anywhere near my flowers. So stay away. And I'm not letting you be alone with them, either."

She picked him up and carried him into her bedroom where she changed into an old T-shirt and sweat pants. Back in the kitchen, she poured herself a large glass of merlot, then put on an album and settled on a stool in front of the buckets as the full-bodied sounds of the Brooklyn Tabernacle Choir filled the room. Gina drank, and felt herself begin to relax. She would take her time, it was all going to be fine. It was only a practice flower show, right?

Suddenly, Bad Guy pounced on all fours on the counter, scaring her to death.

"No!" Gina swept him off the counter and threw the cellophane after him hoping that would satisfy him for a while.

She found the glossy picture of the flower arrangement she had tucked inside the Schedule and slowly sipped on the wine. She studied the picture, then the imperfect flowers, and poured another glass.

Gina suddenly wished her mother was there. She would know what to do with the flowers, no matter what they looked like. She'd always been the one with the green thumb. After the divorce, they'd moved to the little house and Gina was sure her mother's gardening days were over. There was no more giant yard or deep flower beds of antique roses and azaleas. Their tiny backyard was made up of broken concrete and the front yard consisted of two small squares of dirt on either side of a broken walkway. Who could garden in that?

But her mother had declared war on the yard and every day she knelt between the dry squares and chopped at the dirt with her trowel.

When the dirt looked like ground meat, she'd bought plants for half-price at the nursery even though it meant tuna casserole for dinner and sleeping without air conditioning to pay for them. Her mother had chopped, watered, and fertilized, until one day, Gina came home from school and there were flowers blooming along the broken sidewalk. That was the first time she noticed that theirs was the only house on the block with real flowers.

Gina sat in the kitchen while the choir sang and pictured her mother in a wide-brimmed straw hat, her back rounded over the beds while sitting on a little red stool with flowers blooming all around her. Gina looked at her buckets of wilted carnations and roses and wished she'd asked for help.

CHAPTER 24

At midnight, Gina fell onto the couch, exhausted. The wine was gone and flowers were scattered from the kitchen counter to the base of the balcony door where she had thrown them against the glass. But there were also flowers rising from her container in a beautiful arrangement.

Gina's heart swelled with pride. She had actually done it and just like the *Schedule* instructed. If she tilted her head just so, her flowers lined up in sort of a symmetrical arch, more or less. She'd used an odd number of each kind, placing a big one in the middle, and the highest part of the arrangement was one and a half times the height of the container. She had done everything just like the Schedule said.

Gina had chosen a glass vase. It was sixteen inches tall and shaped like a squeezed tube of toothpaste. It rose in an upward twist of blended colors and reminded her of melted crayons. It had been a gift from her father the day she graduated from the academy, and she had forgotten about it until she started looking for a container. She'd found it behind the jug of bleach in the cabinet over the dryer.

Bad Guy started circling again. He'd been satisfied with the cellophane, but now he was standing on his hind legs against the island, stretching his overweight self to get a better look, sniffing the air hungrily.

"No," Gina yelled. The cat dropped back down on all fours and gave her a dirty look.

Gina put a handful of cut stems into the trash, then circled the arrangement, screwing up her eyes, looking for flaws. Something was wrong. She heard Henry's voice in her head saying, 'your arrangement is too thin! Filler, filler, filler!' Then she remembered the potted plants by the elevators.

It was after midnight. Gina was braless under an old T-shirt. She'd already washed her face and applied some special cream that promised to eliminate a pimple that had appeared over her left eye. She peeked out into the hallway. As expected, it was like the mall after hours, sterile and vacuous.

Gripping her clippers, Gina tiptoed out into the hall toward the elevators. The plants by the elevators were enormous. No one would ever notice if she took a few strands. She began snipping and when her hands were full, she tiptoed back to her door and turned the knob. But the knob would not turn. The door had locked behind her.

"Shoot!" Gina cursed out loud. How could she be so stupid? "Shoot," she said again. She glanced at Mrs. Stein's door and noticed the wreath had changed to a grapevine wreath with little birds wired into it.

"Mrs. Stein?" With the ivy trailing everywhere, Gina knocked softly with the back of her hand, then gave the door several sharp raps. She waited, listening, but there was only the quiet background music in the hallway. She glanced at Blake's door, knocked again on Mrs. Stein's door. Still no answer. She had no choice but to try Blake's.

"Yes?" Immediately, the sound of his voice came from deep inside the apartment.

"Blake?" Gina called loudly into the door. "I'm so sorry to bother you, it's me, Gina," then she blurted out in one breath, "I've locked myself out no need to open the door but could you please call downstairs and ask the concierge to come up and let me in thank you."

"What?" His voice was closer now.

Gina covered the peephole with a finger.

"No need to open up, I'm locked out and I just need you to call downstairs and ask them to come up." The door opened.

Blake looked like a knight in shining armor. He wore a white shirt and there was a glow around his body from the light behind him. He was taller than she remembered and she suddenly felt like Eve, naked and ashamed. She tried covering herself with the ivy.

"I'm so sorry. I'm locked out."

He opened the door a little wider and took a step toward her. She stepped back. His eyes were the color of steel, not brown like she'd remembered. He had old man eyes with heavy lids and there was that small scar across one brow she was starting to love.

"No problem. What's that?" he asked, nodding at her greenery.

"What? Oh, this, nothing. Could you please call downstairs for me? Tell them 12E, no, B," she corrected herself, nodding down the hall. Gina began backing herself toward her condo. "I'll just wait by my door."

"No, wait," he said, opening his door wider. "I've been meaning to call."

She shifted the ivy and clippers to one hand and casually tried wrapping her hair behind her ears. Since their last encounter on the balcony, she hadn't seen or heard from him but she wasn't expecting to. He knew she was preoccupied. But he'd been thinking about her. Gina blushed.

"Really?"

"Yeah, really."

"Doing a little gardening?" he asked, eyeballing the lopsided plants at the elevator.

"What? No, no, I guess, not really. Oh, whatever, I've got to get back in my condo..." Gina suddenly froze. Her head jerked to face her condo.

"Would you like to come inside?" Blake began, but Gina was already pounding on her door.

"Bad Guy! No!" she yelled into the door, then back to Blake. "Call downstairs!" She yelled at the door again. "Stop that!"

"What's wrong?"

Gina pressed her ear to the door.

"Here, kitty, kitty," she called, her voice thick with kindness. She listened again.

"What?" Blake was now standing behind her.

"Bad Guy? Please?" Gina's hands pressed against the door and her face against the wood. "Please, Bad Guy, please don't eat my flowers," she begged, then suddenly she pulled back and yelled at the door. "Get over here!"

Blake took her shoulders. Gina instinctively elbowed him in the stomach and he doubled over, coughing.

"I'm so sorry," Gina said, turning to help. "I didn't mean to do that." Long strands of ivy flailed in the air. "My cat's in there destroying my flowers and he can't because I don't have any more flowers!" Her voice cracked and she was afraid she might start crying. She turned back to the door and pounded.

"Please, Blake, go make the call."

"Okay," he said, "but that hurt."

It seemed like forever, but it was probably just one minute, before Blake reappeared. The elevator chimed and Gina stood behind the concierge's shoulder while he unlocked her door. The second the bolt withdrew, she pushed him aside and rushed inside, her eyes scanning the counter.

"Oh, thank God," Gina said, weak with relief. Everything was exactly the same. Bad Guy was sprawled in his usual repose on the couch.

"Is everything okay?" the concierge asked from the doorway. Blake was watching from a safe distance behind him.

"Everything is fine," Gina whispered, then gently closed the door.

CHAPTER 25

Saturday morning, Gina placed her arrangement in the passenger seat so she could hold it with one hand and steer with the other. Mona's house was not that far. If she drove slowly, she should be fine.

She held the wheel steady and shifted into drive. The car circled upward through the underground parking garage. Gina resisted the urge to hurry. It was almost six-thirty and every second in the car was a second lost to primp her arrangement at Mona's before having to be out of the house. The Jeep emerged from the garage, and there was a deafening crash as a wall of rain hit the windshield like a guillotine blade.

Gale force winds rocked the car. With the wipers on high, Gina kept a death grip on the wheel and the other on the vase as her eyes scanned the road. Lightning and thunder flipped the sky back and forth like a light switch and she shuddered with each deafening crash. Even with the wipers on high she could barely see the car ahead. The flooded curbs kept everyone looking for higher ground which meant most of the cars were trying to stay in the center of the road no matter which way they were going.

Gina swerved to miss an oncoming car and water from the vase sloshed over her hand. The flowers began working themselves out of the container but there wasn't anything she could do about it. She felt herself start to panic but she only had a few blocks to go. Then she saw flashing lights at the intersection up ahead. Several stalled cars were blocking the street. Her eyes darted from the intersection to the rising water, and in an instant, she slammed on the accelerator. The motor raced and the car surged through the high water and around the stalled cars.

Gina felt relieved once she'd cleared the intersection. Then she realized she'd used both hands on the steering wheel. The flowers now covered the floor of the car, the whole arrangement was upside down. She wanted to scream, but there was nothing she could do but keep driving.

Gina stopped at the flooded curb in front of Mona's house. The rain was blowing sideways as she raced around to the passenger side of the car and began stuffing flowers back into the vase. Up and down the street other daughters were doing the same thing. She grabbed her small bag of supplies and ran like a maniac for the house.

Several mothers met her at the door and handed her a towel then Gina hurried to find her place. Her name was written on a small card on top of a small table in one of the bedrooms. Gina set the container down, then did her best to recreate the arrangement. She had just finished re-stuffing the ivy when she heard Charlotte's voice and the clapping of hands.

"Alright, ladies, out, out, out. The judges are waiting in the kitchen." Charlotte's face appeared at the door. "Time to go, dear. You don't want to be here when the judges start. You'll be disqualified."

"I know, I know. I'm almost done."

"Well, hurry up." Charlotte continued to move slowly down the hall with her message.

Gina caught up with the others at the front door then remembered she'd left her purse in the kitchen.

Helen caught her arm. "We're going for coffee at Raymond's. Can you go?"

"Sure. I just have to get my purse from the kitchen. I'll see you there." The coffee shop was close by.

Gina entered the kitchen and was surprised to see her mother and Mona talking with a thin young man in baggy shorts. His forearms were covered in tattoos and they had just reached for two large grocery sacks sitting on Mona's counter. The sacks looked very familiar. They locked eyes and suddenly, he was gone with both of them.

Without thinking, Gina began to chase him, but collided with Mona instead.

"You shouldn't be back here. You know you'll be disqualified if the judges see you."

Gina ignored her and took two steps at a time down the back stairs, then dashed around the corner of the house, just in time to see the man throw the sacks into the trunk of a green Dart.

"Stop!" she yelled, running across Mona's front yard, then stood in the rain and watched the Dart drive away.

"Who was that?" Gina asked when she got back to the kitchen. Claire handed her a dry towel.

"That was Jonas," said Mona, "he's a distant nephew."

"I bet."

"Shhhh," interrupted her mother. "It's alright, Gina."

"Don't shush me, Mom. I know what that was. You're supposed to be getting out of the business."

"Shhhh," her mother said again.

"Please, Mom. You said you were getting out of the business. I should have arrested him."

"Do you have your badge?" asked Mona.

Gina reached in her pocket, before remembering she was wearing her sweats.

Ruby walked in and her eyes lit up at the sight of Gina.

"Hello," she said, before catching the look in Mona and Claire's eyes.

"I'll just get myself some coffee and start in on the lunch, don't mind me at all."

Mona took back the towel from Gina and replaced it with her purse, leading her in the direction of the dining room.

"Time to go, Gina. We'll see you for lunch. Ta ta." But just as they got to the dining room, Mona suddenly remembered something and caught Gina's collar, pulling her back.

"I forgot, the judges are here. You should leave through the kitchen door. Now shoo."

"I swear she looked a hundred," Helen was saying as Gina joined them at the coffee shop. They all looked exhausted, in a homeless kind of way, with strands of hair hanging in their faces and dark circles under their eyes.

"One was using a walker and the other one must have been ninety," Brooke added.

"Who are we talking about?" asked Gina, taking a seat.

"The judges. The one with the walker was Mrs. Wicker," continued Brooke. "Mother says she's been judging flower shows for at least fifty years."

"Gina," said Helen, "we're going to have a party Friday night at my house. A picnic, nothing fancy. Can you come? You can bring someone."

"I'll bring potato salad and deviled eggs," Brooke volunteered, then asked Gina, "can you bring a dessert?"

"Okay. But listen, I think we have a problem. I just caught the moms sending off some sacks of weed with a kid. I think he's going to deliver them to The Village."

"I can't believe it. They have so much nerve," said Brooke. "When are they going to quit?"

"That's a good question," said Gina.

"I can bring Texas trash," said Sheralyn, still thinking about the picnic. "Who are you going to bring, Gina? What about that guy that picked you up from Mona's?"

"Maybe. I'm not sure if he'd come."

"Do you want me to ask Bryan if he knows anyone?" Sheralyn asked.

"No, thanks. I'll figure it out."

Sheralyn was about to protest but Helen touched Brooke's arm and nodded across the coffee shop. "Don't look now, but there's our competition, the Goldenrods."

The two women had already drawn the attention of the whole coffee shop as they walked toward the girls' table. Their creased white tennis shorts barely covered their long, tan legs.

"Brooke?" asked the taller of the two.

"Hi Beverly," said Brooke.

"I almost didn't recognize you. Are those your pajamas?"

"Sweat pants. We had an early morning meeting."

"What about?"

Gina shifted in her seat.

"Oh, nothing," said Brooke, then included Gina. "Beverly is a Goldenrod."

At the mention of the rival garden club, Gina rolled her eyes.

"That's nice," Gina said into her coffee.

"Thank you," Beverly gushed. "We've been trying to get Brooke to join us for years."

"Mother would kill me."

"Tell them you're never going to join. You're too young. I'm sure they'd understand."

"No, Beverly, they would kill us," said Sheralyn.

"Why?"

"Because they think you cheated at the last flower show," said Gina.

Beverly's engineered mouth hardened as she stared at Gina. "I'm sorry, who are you?"

"This is Gina Sessions," volunteered Brooke. "Her mother is Claire Sessions," then added, almost as an afterthought, "Gina's a daughter."

Her cold eyes narrowed as Beverly's jaw muscles worked into knots just under her perfect skin. She smiled politely, then straightened herself and adjusted her purse over her shoulder. Gina stopped her.

"Excuse me, but is that a Fendi?"

"What?"

"Is your purse a Fendi? I really like it. I've been looking for something just like it and I'd love to know where you got it."

"The mall somewhere, I can't remember. Sorry," she added, not looking sorry at all.

"That's too bad," said Gina. "You sure?"

Beverly pretended to think about it. "Extremely sure," then she gave them all a sweeping smile. "Sorry to interrupt, ladies. Nice to see you, Brooke. Helen." She ignored the others and then turned and left the coffee shop as if she were working a runway.

"The moms are right," said Gina, raising her coffee to her lips. "They definitely cheated, and they'll probably do it again."

CHAPTER 26

Cars began pulling up to the valet stand in front of Mona's house. The rain had stopped and the sun was shining.

"Perfect timing," said Mona as she watched from one of the living room windows. Sounds coming from the kitchen told them the judges were leaving with their thank you gifts and boxed lunches.

"Here they come," said Claire, as the girls got closer. "I don't know about you but I'm hiding in the butler's pantry." Quickly she retreated to the small space between the kitchen and dining room where she'd have an excellent shot of the entry, living room, dining room and den. Most of the other mothers followed.

Claire wanted to stay hidden until Gina had had time to see the judges' comments about her arrangement. After that, she'd casually appear to pick up the pieces. That's what most of the mothers planned on doing, too.

Gina walked through the front door and disappeared through the entry and into the living room. Claire almost didn't recognize her. She was wearing a pale orange dress with matching pumps and her dark hair was piled high in a swept up arrangement. She looked so beautiful. Trancelike, Claire left the huddle of mothers and pushed past a growing crowd of guests, dodging waiters serving mimosas.

As she rushed to follow her daughter, she saw Brooke, Helen, and Sheralyn ahead of her. They'd already found Gina and Claire suddenly pulled back and decided to watch from the door.

"You got a ribbon!" Sheralyn applauded, taking the silky piece of fabric from Gina's hands.

"White," sighed Gina.

"Hey, you should be proud," said Helen. "At least you got one."

"White's a loser color. They give it to you so you won't feel bad."

"That's not true," said Sheralyn, "because all I got was a sticker. For participation, or something like that. They probably felt like they had to give me something since I used so many flowers."

"What did your card say?" Gina held up her own three-by-five card with the judges' comments and began reading, *Please,* 'and it's underlined,' Gina said, *thoroughly check the condition of your flowers. Some could have been improved with a little more pruning. Others were in poor condition. Container, however, is beautiful and worth spending a little more money on flowers.'*

"They said that?" said Sheralyn.

"True, though."

Sheralyn pulled her card from her pocket and began reading in a dramatic voice, "We certainly felt your creative juices going, however, a little less greenery, a little more structure, and please refer to pages 22 and 23 in the Schedule for specific instructions regarding composition."

"How did you do?" Gina asked Brooke.

"I got a white, too."

"I didn't even get a sticker," said Helen.

"We're doomed," said Gina.

"What?" said Claire, leading with her cane as she pushed her way into their circle.

"Hi, Mom. I guess we didn't do so well," laughed Gina.

"You think it's funny, do you? You certainly won't be laughing when the Goldenrods win the Excelsior! You want us to cooperate with your other demands and hardly even try? The Goldenrods are trying, I can tell you that."

"Mom!" Gina said, embarrassed. "We tried."

Claire braced herself, knowing she was treading dangerously close to the edge, but plowed ahead.

"I thought you wanted to win."

"Of course we want to win, and we definitely want the silver," said Sheralyn.

"This was our first show," said Gina.

"Then I'd say you have a lot of work to do because in two weeks, the judges won't be one hundred years old." Claire gripped her cane and shifted her weight, looking into each of their eyes. "We need to work together."

She was surprised when Gina kept silent.

"Consider this your warning. Do what you want with it but you'll have no one to blame but yourselves if the Goldenrods win."

The silence was painful. Claire thought she might have gone too far when Sheralyn blinked her doe-like eyes and answered in a sincere voice, "Yes, ma'am."

"Okay," sighed Brooke. "I'll admit it. I've been winging most of this. Come on, Helen, I guess we better go figure something out." Claire and Gina watched them leave and then they were alone in the room. The crowd in the hallway was also thinning—a sign that lunch would be soon.

"Well?"

"Well what?" said Gina.

"Are you going to try?"

"Hey, at least I got a white ribbon. Not everybody got a ribbon."

"They gave it to you for the container."

"They did not."

"Yes they did. I heard the judges talking."

"Okay, maybe. But that's because my flowers fell over in my car, it was really hard getting them back in and it was raining so bad. It won't happen again."

"But that's exactly what I'm trying to tell you! If you'd called me and asked for help, I would have told you the vase will always fall over in the car unless you've got it in some kind of box. It happened to me at my first flower show. I want to help you, Gina. We won't win if we don't work together. And if we don't win, the rest is going to be a fight and I think you know what I mean."

Gina seemed to understand. They were running out of time and there was more than the Excelsior at stake.

The dinner bell tinkled from the dining room.

"Oh good, lunch must be ready," Claire added. "I want to get a good table."

CHAPTER 27

After lunch, Gina left Mona's and drove directly to The Village. She'd had the idea over lunch. If Jonas was delivering those sacks of weed, maybe she could find them before Mr. Crawley did. She parked behind the main building near a side entrance marked with a wooden plaque that said "Family." Gina watched a short line of men and women holding onto walkers shuffle into a waiting van. The scene reminded her of the movie *Cocoon*. A somber tune played from the bell tower of a nearby Catholic church.

"Can you please tell me where Mr. Jones' room is?" Gina asked at the nurses' station.

"Room 202," answered a nurse without looking up.

Gina went straight and then right down a long hall. She tried not to look right and left where rows of the grey-haired sat in wheelchairs, waiting. Waiting for what, she had no idea. But they were there, waiting. As she walked down the hall, she noticed that every door was open and every TV blared on high.

Half-way down the hall, Gina jumped when a tiny woman threw up her hand and shouted, "I've got to go to the bathroom!"

Gina wasn't sure she was talking to her but then she waved at her wildly and said it again.

"Okay, okay," said Gina, "just a minute." Gina hurried back to the nurses' station.

"Excuse me, there's a lady down the hall in a wheelchair, says she needs to use the restroom?"

"Is she a tiny little thing with a green blanket over her legs?"

"I think so."

"She wears a diaper, honey. She don't need no bathroom," then the phone rang and Gina lost her attention to a call.

"Someone is coming right now to take you," Gina lied once she'd returned to the little lady. It seemed to satisfy her.

Gina tapped on Room 202 and a man's voice asked her to come in.

It was a long narrow room and in one corner was a white curtain hanging from a stainless bar attached to the ceiling. Beneath the curtain she could see four steel legs.

Mr. Jones was watching TV from a chair. He was a handsome man and was dressed in pressed blue jeans, slippers and a flannel shirt. A few bits of hair were neatly combed to the side and a walker stood parked in a corner. Gina recognized the theme song from *Bonanza*.

"Good morning, Mr. Jones," she said from the doorway, "my name is Officer Sessions. Can I come in?"

"Call me Jonesy," he said, then pointed the remote at the TV and clicked it a few times until the sound had lowered.

Gina pulled over a chair and sat facing him. She noticed he had cloudy brown eyes and a thin, angular face. His hands, folded neatly in his lap, were cold-looking, but his smile was warm and alive. She could tell he liked visitors, especially female ones. Gina found herself smiling back.

"What did you say your name was?" he asked.

"Gina Sessions. Officer Sessions."

"Woohoo, are you going to arrest me?"

"Should I?"

"Hello?" a man's voice yelled from behind the curtain. "Is someone there?"

Mr. Jones rolled his eyes.

"Who's there?" The voice was loud and demanding.

"Hello, I'm visiting Mr. Jones," Gina spoke up.

"Are you family?"

"Oh, shut up, Craig," said Mr. Jones. "He'll talk your ear off if you get him started, so don't."

"I've been here five years," the voice continued loudly. "I was in an accident in 1993 and so I live here. I was just taking a nap. Are you the daughter?"

"Mind your own business, Craig!" shouted Mr. Jones.

"It's alright," said Gina. "I'm just visiting, Craig. I'm going to talk to Mr. Jones now..."

"Oh, that's okay. I'm not sleeping."

Gina lowered her voice so that only Mr. Jones could hear.

"Do you know why I'm here?"

"Nope."

"Mr. Crawley called me. He's worried." She leaned forward, clasped her hands, and rested them on her knees. "I need your help."

"Not sure if I can help you. I'm 89, you know." Then he winked at her.

Gina adjusted in her chair. "Mr. Crawley thinks someone is selling marijuana to the residents. Is that true?"

Mr. Jones pretended to be surprised. But just as he was about to continue, a male attendant entered and with barely a nod to Gina or Mr. Jones, he disappeared behind the curtain. Sounds of metal and grunts were enough to tell her the male nurse was helping Craig with a bed pan. She and Mr. Jones sat in awkward silence.

"Sorry about that," said Craig loudly as the attendant sprayed an aerosol.

Gina continued.

"Mr. Jones, what do you know about the weed?"

"I'd like to know where I can get some."

"I'm not kidding, Mr. Jones. You know you're not too old to get arrested and Mr. Crawley is pretty sure about his suspicions."

"That guy is from New York. What does he think he knows?"

"What do you think he knows?"

The old man stared at his fingernails and Gina noticed a slight tremor. "I have no idea."

Sounds of teeth brushing came from behind the curtain. Gina got up and walked to the dresser where three pictures were displayed in a neat row. The first was a young couple with a child. The second was an old wedding photo and the third was a picture of several small children.

"Are these your great-grandkids?"

"Yep. They're ten and twelve, I think. Good kids."

"Is this your son?

"That's him and his wife. They live out of state."

"How long have you lived here, Mr. Jones?"

"Ten years. I broke my back, couldn't drive anymore and couldn't fix my meals so after my wife died, the kids brought me here." His eyes drifted up to the TV. "I've been here a long time, but it got a whole lot better about five years ago."

Gina waited while they stared at one another.

"Do you like it here?" she asked.

"It's alright," he shrugged. "It's the last place most of us will live, so we try to make the best of it. Don't you think that's a good idea?"

"Maybe," she said. "But someone may get hurt. Have you thought about that?"

"Would you like to know my opinion?" a voice shouted from the other side of the room.

"No, we wouldn't, Craig, so shut up," shouted Mr. Jones back, then to Gina he said, "If you mean someone may die, it's kind of what we're all hoping for, if it's our time, of course."

Gina thought she saw his eyes twinkle. She liked the old man and wished she could just let him be. Neither of them wanted to be there. Gina took her seat in the chair again.

"Mr. Jones, I don't care, really, about what you choose to do at this stage in your life. But I'm a police officer and it's my job. Mr. Crawley could get in a lot of trouble. He's supposed to protect people. He could lose his job. And someone could get hurt. There are a lot of reasons why you need to tell me where the marijuana is coming from."

His eyes blinked slowly. "I'm sorry, honey, but there's nothing going on here that needs protecting. And if there were, I'm sure I wouldn't know the details. We're all good. Honestly. So, are you from Dallas?"

"Don't try to change the subject. I just want to catch the bad guys."

"Like I said, there aren't any bad guys here."

"I wish that were true," Gina said, suddenly thinking about the mothers. She felt her pager vibrate. It was the Captain. She called the office from Mr. Jones' phone.

"Where are you?" her boss asked.

Gina told him.

"Wrap it up. There's been another robbery in your old neighborhood and Jacobs is on vacation. I know you aren't senior but since you've been working so closely with Jacobs, I thought you might like to run it. We're pretty sure it's the same group."

Gina put the receiver back in the cradle then pushed her chair back to the wall. He looked disappointed.

"I have to go, Mr. Jones, but I'll be back. Thank you, even though you haven't been very helpful."

"Time to go already?" the voice asked from behind the curtain. "It sure has been nice talking to you. Come back anytime."

"I will," said Gina. She looked at Mr. Jones. He rolled his eyes, then looked up at the TV.

Gina heard the volume go up as soon as she was back in the hall.

CHAPTER 28

"I have a surprise for you," Claire sang, knocking firmly on Gina's door. She fumbled with the box in her arms as well as her purse and cane, trying to check her watch. It was already 7:00 a.m. Monday morning and she was going to be so mad at herself if Gina had already left for work.

A door opened down the hall and a handsome man leaned out.

"Everything okay?"

"This is my daughter's apartment. I'm her mother. I'm not sure why she isn't answering but I'm sure everything's all right. She's a police officer. She has a gun."

He came toward her with long easy strides, smiling as he reached out his hand.

"Hello," he said, "I'm her neighbor, Blake."

Claire juggled the box and took his hand.

"You know Gina?"

"We've met a few times."

"Well, so nice to meet you. I didn't know Gina knew any of her neighbors, but now that I've said that it makes her sound like a hermit, which she's not, but I'm so glad to meet you. I think it's wonderful when neighbors in apartments get to know each other, especially when no one has a backyard."

"It's a condo, Mom," Gina said from behind her. "Hello, Blake."

"Hi."

"Oh, honey, you're home," she said, and then she was suddenly pulled inside by her sweater. Gina shut the door in the face of the good-looking man.

"What is wrong with you?" Claire said, nearly falling over her cane.

"Nothing," Gina said, then tried to be helpful by taking the heavy box.

"No, no, I've got it, but was that the same man that picked you up from the flower show?"

"Yes, and what are you doing here so early?" Gina's hair was tied in a ponytail and there were deep creases on her face. She'd obviously been asleep.

"I think your bell is broken. I've been standing in the hall for five minutes."

"It's working. I thought you were selling something and was hoping you'd go away."

Claire followed her into the kitchen.

"I didn't sleep very well last night, Mom, and I'm working on a case." Papers were still spread across the kitchen island.

Claire set the box on the counter, then sat down on one of the bar stools and accepted a cup of coffee.

"I was hoping I could catch you before work. I wanted you to have this." Claire was momentarily distracted as her eyes roamed around the kitchen and living area. They stopped on the bookshelves that lined a wall.

"Okay, so what is it?"

"Blake is so handsome."

Gina poured cat food into a large bowl. The sound drew the cat out of the bedroom.

"That is the fattest animal I have ever seen in my life. Do you have to walk it?"

"No, Mom, it's a cat," said Gina.

"So who is he?"

"Bad Guy."

"Not the cat. I mean Blake. What does he do?"

"He's an artist, but that's about all I know because I've been so busy with work and the flower show. It's actually a little awkward. Hopefully once this thing is over, he won't think I'm too crazy and I can go back to a normal life. I don't know. So what's in the box?"

"Have you heard anything about the promotion?"

"No, Mom. I told you I would let you know as soon as I heard anything."

"Weren't you supposed to hear last Friday? Do you think something is wrong?"

"I don't know."

"Well, this is just ridiculous. They shouldn't make you wait like this. Isn't there someone you can call? I could still ask Mona to call."

"Definitely not."

"Well, what about the Captain? Can't he check on the grade for you?"

Gina dropped her head into the palms of her hands, muffling her words. "He doesn't have anything to do with them, Mom. Anyway, maybe I didn't pass." She raised her head. "Please, let's not talk about this. Can you just tell me about that box so I can go to work?"

Gina looked so tired. Claire wished it were normal to put her arms around her but anything like that would defeat the purpose.

"I'm sure you passed. But if you didn't, we'll just keep it on the prayer list. You'll get it next year."

Gina smiled weakly and lifted the mug to her lips.

"So, to the reason I came by."

Claire worked open the lid on the box and took out a small wooden chest about the size of a shoe box. It had a rounded top and a brass catch that turned easily. She lifted the lid. Inside were several smaller boxes, envelopes and loose things which she then lay on the counter between them.

"Go ahead," Claire said, motioning toward one of the boxes.

Gina hesitated, then chose one and worked off the fitted top. Inside were colorful metal shapes and fabrics. She held up a small pin of tarnished wings with a short ribbon attached.

"They are your father's medals from the Korean War," said Claire. "I think you should have them."

Claire felt her chest tighten as she watched Gina remove the items, one by one, and gingerly place the familiar things on the counter in organized rows. Several medals, bars and ribbons to name the battles, then papers - one saying he'd graduated from flight school, another commending him for his service, sending him home. There were letters home to his mother, and then to her. Not once did Gina look at her mother. Soon, the box was empty.

"I never knew you had all this," Gina said, rubbing her thumb over the stamped brass. "Why have I never seen it?"

"I'd forgotten about it," Claire said, "but the other day when I was looking for containers in the attic, there it was. Just popped right out at me and I thought, 'This needs to go to Gina,' especially after our talk the other day. I want you to be proud of him." Claire stared at the medals. She had come to say something else. "I'm sorry for saying things that upset you. I rarely say the right thing, and I'm sorry. I wish I could help."

Seconds passed. She was surprised when Gina put her arm around her shoulders.

"Thank you. I am proud of him."

They separated.

"I recognized the vase you used at the flower show. He was very proud of you, too."

Gina stared silently at the things on the counter.

"Well, I need to let you go to work." Claire began to edge herself off her stool.

"Wait, Mom," Gina said. "I'm going to stay home today. Can you stay a little while and help me? I want to try and rework my arrangement. But if you want, we can go to the florist and get some more flowers. Just let me get dressed." Gina talked as she disappeared into the bedroom.

"What about work?"

"I can take a half- day. I worked this weekend so it shouldn't be a problem. And I need the practice."

"Okay," Claire said, smiling to herself. "While you're getting dressed, I'll piddle around out here." She eyed the disorganized bookcases.

"I'll only be a second. Don't touch anything."

For the next few hours, they systematically pulled out the worst of the flowers as Claire explained what the judges had been looking for. She showed Gina why there were too many angles in the arrangement and too many flowers. It needed a focal point, an anchor, and certain flowers worked, others didn't. Claire worked quickly as Gina watched.

And then she was finished and they both took a step back. The change was startling, even to Claire as she pulled at a microscopic piece of greenery.

"Do you have any more of this greenery?" Claire asked.

Gina suddenly burst out laughing, then told her about Friday night when she'd cut the ivy at the elevators, gotten locked out, all the screaming at Bad Guy with Blake looking over her shoulder.

By noon, they'd done several arrangements.

"These are good," said Claire, standing back to look at the new ones. "Now I've got to go."

Gina stopped her at the door. The expression on her face told Claire it was serious.

"Mom, you need to tell me what's going on with the other business. You've got a plan, right? We are less than two weeks away from the flower show but I don't think I can keep you safe much longer."

Claire shrugged, not looking up. "I don't know what to tell you, Gina. Mona said she would take care of it. She may wait to see how well we do at the show. Don't worry, it will be fine."

Gina pressed her hands together. "Mom, please, I'm begging you, don't wait. You have got to get out of the business. I'm talking with the people at The Village. I'm afraid of what I'm going to find out."

Claire looked at her watch. "I need to go. I've got a lot of things on my list today. I think you're doing great. I'll see you later."

"This isn't *Arsenic and Old Lace*, you know. You will get caught."

Claire laughed. "Don't worry, no one is going to find out."

"Too late," Gina said, pushing back her hair in frustration.

Claire stopped at the door. "What do you mean?"

"That's all I can say, but someone is going to talk and then my hands are tied, only I'll probably get arrested too because I knew about it."

Claire was shocked. "Who is talking about it?"

"That's not the point, Mom, and I couldn't tell you anyway. Please talk to Mona. Tell her it's time to start throwing stuff away."

Claire studied Gina. "I will but she won't listen. I just handle the money, you know."

"Then I'm going to Mona's and, I swear, Mom, I'll clean out the closet myself. I know she's the queen bee and she tells everyone else what to do, but she can't thumb her nose at the law and right now, I'm the law."

The second she got home, Claire dialed Mona's number.

"Mona, I think we should start throwing stuff away. Someone at The Village is talking." She listened for a minute.

"No, Gina hasn't told anyone, but she sounded very serious that we might not have as much time as we thought. I don't know, but maybe they know more than we think."

She listened again, longer this time. "Mona, listen to me. I think she might be coming to your place. Soon."

There was a pause.

"I'm on my way."

CHAPTER 29

Gina drove to the office. She thought about going straight to Mona's but decided to give it more thought. That was a confrontation she wanted to be prepared for.

When she stepped off the elevator, she saw that most of the floor was still at lunch. Across the room in his glass office her boss looked up and immediately motioned for her to come to him. Gina reluctantly obeyed.

One of the rookies with a tight crew cut was finishing his lunch at his desk. On her way to the Captain's, Gina stopped to ask a favor. She'd had an idea.

"Hey Brad, can I borrow your squad car, just for the afternoon?"

"Sure, Gina. Just grab the keys when you need it. I'm in court all afternoon."

"Perfect."

"Close the door," the Captain said as she entered his office.

She focused on a plaque above his head and waited. He slowly leaned back in his leather chair and did a tapping thing with his hands, elbows resting on the arms of his chair, fingertips touching.

"Nice of you to stop by, Sessions. Since I've been calling you all morning and you don't answer, there must be some special occasion going on away from the office that I don't know about."

"Sorry, Captain, I needed to take some personal time. You know I worked almost the whole weekend."

Ignoring her answer, he leaned forward and threw something at her. It landed on the desk. "Here."

She picked up the folded sheet of paper and scanned the first lines.

"It says I scored a 95," Gina said.

"Congratulations."

"I passed?" Gina grinned. "I passed!" She was practically giggling.

The Captain wiped at a smile. "I hear five other guys scored just as good."

"What does that mean?"

"It means there are six of you competing for the same position." He picked up a pencil and began twirling it through his fingertips. "I've done what I can, Sessions, despite my better judgment. I still think you need more experience, but if they think you can do it, I think you should have the chance, but," he added, bowing his head over his own paperwork, "don't expect too much. Now go on, get something done today. And by the way, I want that drug thing at The Village wrapped up. Either figure out if it's true or find the supplier. I don't want the Mayor finding out his mother are getting high at the retirement center and we can't seem to stop them. Now get out of here."

She backed away toward the door.

"Thank you, sir, thank you. You'll see. This job is mine."

He grumbled. "I assume you have someone to share your good news with?"

"My mo..." and then she stopped. "I'll think of someone. Thank you, sir."

Gina opened the door and the room erupted in cheers. She didn't know where everyone came from but her friends and coworkers had all been waiting for her and were all clapping and throwing her high fives. Gina held up the paper and pumped her fist. She felt like Rocky, at the top of the stairs.

Gina was still feeling the high as she headed for The Village again. The days were growing hotter, and she dreaded what she was about to do. She hoped it wouldn't take long.

She parked the car outside the family entrance and waited. Two long hot hours passed, before the green Dart pulled into the parking lot. She was drenched in sweat as she watched Mona's nephew get out. He adjusted his baggy shorts up over his boxers and tightened his belt, then took off his cap and used his fingers to comb through his hair. Finally, he stubbed out a cigarette and pulled a plump grocery sack from the back of the car.

As soon as he disappeared, she followed him inside. She watched as he turned the first corner. She caught up just in time to see him chatting with the nurses like they were old friends before heading down the long hallway.

He entered a room at the end of the hall. She thought it could be Mr. Jones' and waited for him to come back out. He was still holding the sack, but he immediately disappeared into another room. This time he came out without the sack.

Gina hurried the opposite way to the open dining room and sat with a resident who was asleep in his wheelchair. As soon as Jonas passed by, Gina retraced her steps to the last room and knocked.

"Come in." She was surprised to hear it was a woman's voice.

Inside was the tiny little lady who'd had her hand in the air. The green blanket was still draped across her legs.

"Hello. I've seen you before haven't I? How nice. My name's Minnie." She extended a twig of an arm to Gina.

"Gina." She was surprised how firmly the child-sized woman gripped her hand.

"Are you Jacob's daughter?"

"Jacob? Oh, you mean Mr. Jones. No, I'm not."

"Oh, that's right, Jonesy told me about you. You are a police officer and you want to know about some heady nuggets."

Gina couldn't hide her surprise at Minnie's use of street slang for good weed. "You got me," she said, raising her hands in defeat. There was no sign of the sack.

"Can you help me out?" Gina asked.

Minnie smiled sweetly. "I'm sorry, dear. I don't know what you're talking about."

"Come on, Minnie. I just saw the kid leaving here without the sack. I know he brought."

Minnie blinked.

"The marijuana?"

"Well, I don't believe I have any marijuana. But if there were any here, I'd say it would be a nice alternative to being put in a circle to kick a ball and call it exercise. The definition of fun doesn't change just because you get old."

Gina studied the old woman. If she had to guess, Minnie was the ring leader. The sweet ones always were.

"Are you sure you don't have anything under that blanket?" Gina asked.

Minnie raised the quilt that covered her legs. Only there were no legs to cover. "Diabetes," she said matter of factly. "It's like leprosy."

"I'm so sorry," Gina said, stumbling over her words.

"My husband moved me here, right before he died. It's a nice place, most of the time. But sometimes, like life, you gotta' make your own fun."

Gina looked away. On the dressing table was a silver-plated brush, comb and hand mirror. A picture of Minnie on her wedding day, some playing cards and a small radio rested beside the mirror.

"Would you mind getting me my sweater out of the closet?" Minnie asked.

Gina opened the door to the closet. There were several to choose from. "Any particular color?"

"Any one will do."

Gina pulled out a pale blue one, then froze. The brown paper sack was on the floor. The adrenaline kicked in as well as her policeman's mind. She'd been asked to look in the closet, discovery wasn't a problem. It was right there, plain as day. Gina picked up the sack and held it in front of Minnie. She forgot about the sweater.

"What is this? If you tell me now, things might go better for you."

Minnie covered her mouth, feigning shock. "Oh dear. You found me out. Go ahead and open it."

Gina unfolded the brown paper. Inside, were two neat stacks of Depends.

"Jonas buys them for me at Wal-Mart and brings them by the dozen. It's much cheaper that way. He's such a nice young man though I know he tries to hide his tattoos. He also smokes which I think is disgusting."

"This is what Jonas delivered today? Depends?"

"Well, I'm not going to the store and buy them for myself! People stare and I know what they're thinking. I have my pride."

Gina closed up the sack and put it back in the closet. The tiny face had a wide grin on it. She'd fallen right into Minnie's hands.

"So I guess everyone else is hiding their Depends?" asked Gina.

Minnie nodded.

"Not marijuana?"

"That's right," she said with an honest smile. "But you might go look in Jessie's room. She always seems to be very happy. Are you married?"

Gina noticed her looking at her ring finger and instinctively covered it. "No. Why should I look in Jessie's room?"

Minnie rolled her chair to the door and called to someone standing in the hall.

"Crystal. What room is the Mayor's mother in?"

"320," came a voice from far away.

Minnie rolled herself back in. "She's in room 320. I think she's very suspicious."

Gina closed her notebook and started to leave then stopped to ask one last question.

"Minnie, can I ask you something? If you use Depends, why were you asking me to take you to the bathroom?"

Minnie wheeled herself closer to Gina. She reached out and took hold of her hand, pulling her lower so that she could look directly into her eyes. It was like looking into a deep well of wisdom.

"Sometimes, I do it for the fun of it," she said. "I like you, Gina, I hope you'll come back for a real visit." She began pressing out the wrinkles in her blanket, which convinced Gina that if she were to dig any deeper, she'd find Minnie in charge of it all.

CHAPTER 30

Gina decided that Minnie and Mona were very much alike. Both were confident, strong women and used to getting what they wanted. Gina had had enough. She'd gone back to the office, tried to work, and finally realized she wasn't going to get anything done until she confronted Mona. It was close to five when Gina knocked boldly on Mona's kitchen door and let herself in.

Cleeve and Mona were both sitting at the kitchen table with a glass of wine. He was hunched over his newspaper, his glasses hanging off the end of his nose, while she was talking on the phone with her feet propped up in the chair next to her.

Gina announced herself as she walked through the kitchen. "I'm going to go check on your silver closet. It's empty isn't it?"

"What?" Mona reached out just in time to catch her by the sleeve.

"I need to see inside the silver closet. I want to know if you've made any progress."

"You can't go back there."

"Why not?"

"It's a mess."

"I doubt that."

"What's a mess?" asked Cleeve. Mona glared at Gina, then turned to her husband.

"Cleeve, would you mind taking your paper out to the porch? I think this is going to be a female discussion."

He thought he understood and quickly folded up his paper and left for the safety of the outdoors.

"Goodness, Gina," Mona said, "we are handling things our way and Cleeve doesn't know."

"You're not handling things the way I meant for you to handle things. Don't you remember, after the flower show? I was there. I *saw* Jonas and the sacks. And today I *saw* Jonas with my own eyes going into The Village, delivering those same sacks. I couldn't find them but I know it was your weed. You and Mom are still selling it."

Mona crossed her arms.

"Stop smirking, Mona, this isn't funny."

Gina didn't think she'd ever been this angry at one of the mothers before. She'd always dreaded their meddling and how they completely ignored how uncomfortable they made her feel when talking over her about her personal life. Occasionally she'd fumed inside when they insisted she be at things, and she'd definitely been mad when she'd discovered the pot. But this was different.

She was done. She'd had it with them refusing to obey any rule that wasn't their own and acting like they were more worried about aphids on their roses than they were about going to jail.

"I want to see your closet, Mona."

"I'm not ready for you to see my closet, Gina."

"Will you ever be ready?"

Mona squeezed her lips tightly together.

Gina went around her. Mona bolted out of her chair and followed. When she got to the closet, Gina stepped quickly into the darkened room then opened the smaller door as she'd done a few days before. She pulled the cord. Immediately she saw that the room was empty and it really was a mess. Wires hung from the ceiling and tubing was scattered all over the floor. But there was nothing living. Someone had cleared things out and in a hurry.

Gina went back out into the hall where Mona stood, smiling.

"You moved it," said Gina.

"Of course I did. Isn't that what you wanted?"

"Then why didn't you just say that.

"I don't like being told what to do."

Gina stared at her with narrowed eyes. "Where did you take it?"

"What do you mean?"

"Where did you move it? I know you didn't throw it away."

Mona rolled her eyes. "Gina. Please. You have nothing to worry about."

"Tell me or I'll tell Cleave."

Mona took in an enormous breath. "You wouldn't!"

They stared at one another.

"Okay, I moved it, but it isn't operational, of course. We will take care of the other closets as soon as possible, as soon as the flower show is over."

"If I see it again, I'm going to arrest you myself."

Mona waved a hand. "Oh, be serious."

"Oh, I'm being serious," Gina said, walking back toward the kitchen, "about as serious as a heart attack. Maybe you should go take a look outside."

Mona's smile evaporated. She hurried around Gina to the kitchen sink where she could see into the front yard.

"What is a police car doing in front of this house? Of my house?"

It was Gina's turn to smile as she took out her badge and laid it on the table.

"Just in case you were wondering whether or not I was serious."

"Move that car out from in front of my house!" Mona demanded.

"I will. I wanted you to know I'll be watching you."

Mona went back to her seat at the table and offered Gina a glass of wine, as if it were just another cocktail hour. Gina wasn't sure if she was on or off duty so she declined.

"I thought we had a deal," Mona said, the tension now gone out of them both. "You agreed that we would give it up after we won the Excelsior."

"You and I both know we won't win. But that's not really what you want, is it?"

"But it's our business..." Mona began, then noticed Gina's exaggerated look toward her badge.

They were silent again.

"Okay," Mona said. "I'll talk to the others. It's such a waste, you know. We have such an efficient system in place, everyone has been very happy with it. What if we just finish delivering what we already have?"

"No," Gina said. "Not another delivery. Not another harvest. Everything stops now."

Mona glared. "If we agree, do you promise you'll still try your best for the Excelsior?"

Gina nodded. "Why don't we both not say anything – but we both do our best to do the right thing."

Cleeve's face appeared at the screen door. Gina noticed he was framed by the trees in their backyard and felt a longing to escape.

"Sorry to interrupt."

"What is it?" Mona asked.

"There's something I needed to talk to you about and I'm about to run to the Club."

Mona looked at Gina. "I think we're done here. What is it?"

"Bryan and I want to take one last hunting trip before the season ends. Is that okay with you?"

"When?"

"This weekend. I promised Bryan he'd get a deer and it's our last chance."

"But what about the picnic Friday night?" She turned to Gina. "You are going to the picnic, aren't you?"

Gina hesitated. "Yes, but how did you know about the picnic?" Mona ignored her and spoke to Cleeve.

"You and Bryan can't miss the picnic, it's at the ranch."

"I know, we won't leave 'til Saturday morning," said Cleeve. "We'll take the plane and still get to the cabin by mid-morning. Bryan says he wants to get home in time for dinner Sunday with Sheralyn and the boys."

Mona shrugged. "That sounds fine to me."

"Okay, good. That's all I wanted to know. So I'm leaving now. Goodbye, ladies."

"Bye, dear."

Cleeve's head disappeared and they heard the sounds of the garage door going up.

"How do you know about the picnic?" Gina asked. She'd already asked Blake if he'd go with her. He'd said yes.

"Charlotte heard Brooke, or maybe it was SueBee, because Helen was talking about it. Someone heard something, oh I don't know. The family picnic is one of our traditions, don't you remember? We had you all out to the ranch almost every year, for ten or fifteen years. So when we heard about your picnic we thought it would be so much fun to do it all again. Don't worry, we'll handle everything."

Gina felt her stomach start to cramp. She'd told Blake it was going to be a quiet get-together of just the daughters. Now it was going to be, at a minimum, lots of people, a buffet, a band, photographers, bartenders and valets.

"But why?" Gina begged.

"You are bringing someone, aren't you?" asked Mona.

"Yes," she sighed. "I'm bringing someone. I told him it would be fried chicken and potato salad at Helen's."

"And now it will be so much more fun. I can't wait to meet him. Does your mother know?"

Cleeve's face appeared at the screen door again.

"Hey, did you know there's a police car parked in our front yard? Some of the neighbors are asking if everything is okay."

CHAPTER 31

Late Friday afternoon the harsh glare that usually reflected off the office building across the street and into her window had faded. The air was still. Traffic noise was getting louder, telling her people were getting an early start on the weekend. The same was true inside as the clock got closer to five and people started closing up their files and sitting on each other's desks.

"Hey Gina, want to go to Hooter's after work?" Brad, the young officer who'd loaned her his car, yelled from across the room.

"No thanks, I'm having my teeth cleaned."

"Come on, good-looking woman like you? Any plans for the evening?"

She ignored him and opened her *Schedule*. She flipped to the last chapter where it talked about the finer points of finishing the arrangement. The big flower show was only one week away and she and the others had been working hard all week.

"By the way, congratulations on passing the test." Brad was now standing beside her, looking over her shoulder. "I know you're going to get it. How many did the Captain say were up for the position?"

Gina closed the book and said quietly, "Six."

"Five others? Really? What do you think your chances are?"

"I'm not really sure, Brad."

"Well, we all think you'd make a great senior detective. Good luck."

He gave her a sincere pat on her shoulder, so she nodded her thanks, then quietly tucked the Schedule back in a drawer. It was time to leave since Blake was picking her up in an hour. She hadn't told him very much about what to expect and her stomach was in knots. She wasn't even sure if he liked to dance.

Gina had been totally surprised when Helen followed through on her idea to host a family picnic. By that evening, everyone had received a phone call and Gina was expected to find a date or they would find one for her. She'd called Blake, assuring him it would be a simple, small backyard picnic. Just a few couples. No big deal.

And then the mothers had heard about it.

With only five days to do everything, they'd mobilized into organizational overdrive. Naturally, tradition dictated that the picnic would be at Cleeve and Mona's ranch, a working ranch outside of Dallas with more than enough room for a dance and bar-b-que. If it rained, they could move everything, including the band, inside.

They got a local restaurant to cater, a country western band was immediately booked, and the girls were told that there would be plenty of things for the grandchildren to do, like four-wheelers, fishing, watching cattle or just going down to the barn to pet the horses. And, oh yes, the girls could help by bringing the desserts.

Gina answered her door holding a Tupperware case of brownies. Blake held out a wrapped package. She didn't know what to say, so he took the Tupperware and she took the gift. It was wrapped in a soft blue tissue. Carefully, she slipped a finger beneath the tape, trying not to tear the paper, and then stared in amazement at the colored pencil drawing of the most gorgeous flower arrangement she could ever imagine.

"I would have brought flowers but decided I should stick with art."

"Thank you," Gina whispered. "It's beautiful."

Blake drove and Gina directed. She was glad he felt like talking. She wanted to learn everything she could about him, but honestly, it was hard to pay attention because she kept thinking how lucky she was to have met someone both nice and good-looking. What made it even harder to concentrate was she got the feeling he liked her. She wanted to keep it that way.

He told her he'd spent four years trying to work in an office, but had finally admitted to himself that all he wanted to do was be a painter. That was at twenty-five, and after that, there had been feast and famine. Mostly feast but plenty of famine. He'd gone to school on the East Coast and he said he really liked dogs and reading and then he looked at Gina and told her he also loved homemade brownies. At least that's what she thought he was saying.

Beyond the city limits, the land rose up in seemingly endless waves. Occasionally they'd roll through a four-way stop with a garage and a feed store. By then the sun was sitting on the edge of the horizon, making it hard to look ahead, so Gina stared out her window at farmhouses and fence lines. Blake craned his neck to look at something, and Gina followed his eyes to see a hawk swooping from a power line before disappearing into the high grass of a field.

"Wow," they both said.

When the paved road turned to gravel, she knew they were on the ranch's private road but there was still no sign of the gate. The sky had become a wash of oranges and blues.

"Hey!" Blake shouted, pointing to the right. Gina looked.

"What?"

"Hay," he said.

"Very funny." She looked again at the map. "Once we cross the second cattle guard, there should be a small ranch house. Then we'll get to a large gated entry made of iron and horns."

"Iron and horns?"

"That's what it says."

"Didn't you used to come out here a lot?"

"Maybe once a year. But that was a long time ago. When we were kids."

In another mile, they began to see cars up ahead. Soon they were part of a line of cars in front and behind them. They knew they were getting close.

"I think I should warn you," Gina began, "I know I told you it was a picnic, but the Garden Club got hold of it and..."

"What does that mean?"

"Well, that means it's going to be a little more complicated. Fancier maybe? Actually, it will probably be over the top. When our mothers found out we were having a picnic, they decided they wanted to recreate the picnics of Garden Club past. Sort of like in Scrooge where you think you must be dreaming and there's lots of people and food and frolic."

"Sounds interesting."

Gina felt like a teenager, completely silly inside. It didn't help that he looked really good in jeans.

"Thanks for coming with me, Blake."

"Thanks for asking." He reached over and squeezed her hand.

"It seems that every time we meet, I'm doing something with my mom. And tonight, well... That's really not all I do. It's this big flower show thing but it will all be over next week. Then my life will return to normal. Or what normal is for me."

"So what's the flower show thing?"

She turned in her seat to face him. "Our mothers have had this club for over fifty years and there's this major contest next week. They were supposed to be retired, but they got it in their heads that they needed to win this trophy one last time. They hate the club that won it last time, and they needed us to help."

"That's nice of you."

"Yeah, well, we didn't volunteer. But that's another story. Anyway, these women have known me my whole life and they will say whatever they feel, so I'm apologizing now. By the way, where were you born?"

"Fort Worth."

Gina was relieved. "Good. If you had said D.C. or California I would have recommended making something up."

The car bounced wildly as they crossed the second cattle guard. The terrain was mowed and the miles of white fencing looked freshly painted. They followed the other cars and drove beneath an elaborate iron gate trimmed in longhorns, where they were met by a man signaling with bright red flags. Soon they were snaking toward a graveled parking area.

"Look," Gina said, pointing. A sprawling hacienda with a red-tiled roof rested on top of a distant hill, giving it 360-degree views of the whole valley.

"Wow," said Blake, "you were right. This is not a normal picnic."

"No, it's not."

Blake and Gina parked. They wandered through the crowd to find the dessert table so she could drop off the brownies. There they found Mona and Charlotte busy re-arranging things.

"Gina!" Charlotte hurried around the table to give her a hug and a loud kiss on the cheek. While still holding on to Gina, her eyes darted to Blake.

"Mona, Charlotte, I'd like for you to meet my neighbor, Blake Downing."

"Thank you for having me," he said, holding out a hand to Charlotte. Mona remained on the other side of the table.

Charlotte let go of Gina and took his hand in both of hers. "We're so glad you came. Have you two been dating long?"

Gina looked at Blake with eyes that said, "I told you so."

"Blake's just my neighbor, Charlotte. He helped me that night I got locked out of my condo when I was getting ready for the flower show. I wanted him to get to meet the reason for all the trouble, and here they are!" She indicated the two mothers. "Oh, I think I hear the band. Blake?" Before she could grasp Blake's hand, Charlotte interrupted.

"Tell us, Blake, where are your people from?"

"Fort Worth."

"Oh, I love Fort Worth!"

"Do you enjoy the museums?" Mona asked, her eyebrows arching high over her sunglasses. The sun had gone down but the grounds around the house were so well lit it still seemed like day.

"Actually, I'm a painter, so I spend a lot of time in museums."

Charlotte put her arm around Gina and squeezed her close. "He's a keeper," she whispered.

"Yes, well, we'll visit with y'all later." Gina ducked out of Charlotte's hug and propelled Blake toward the buffet tables.

"I want to visit more later," Charlotte called after them.

"I want a dance with you both!" Blake waved over his shoulder and Gina pinched his arm.

"Owww. What was that for?"

"Don't make it worse."

"What are you talking about?"

Gina stopped him. "Look over there. See that?" She nodded toward a group of women off in the distance who were obviously studying them.

"They're probably planning our wedding." She let that sink in. "I'm the only one who hasn't been married at least once, out of all the daughters, like I'm cursed or something. They're all praying that I get married before they die and you're just as good as anyone. So if you're smart, you'll not be so charming. You'll thank me later."

"Wow," he said.

"What can I say? I love them. Like I said, it's a curse."

"Okay, but can I at least talk to the men?"

Gina let go of his hand and he left for a group of husbands standing at the top of the hill. Gina found Sheralyn and Bryan at the buffet table, helping their kids load hot dogs onto paper plates.

"Is that him?" asked Sheralyn, nodding toward Blake. He had found the men and a Corona.

"Yep. Blake the neighbor."

Bryan pointed the two little boys in the direction of a child-size picnic table. "Want me to check him out for you?"

"You mean beyond the background check I already ran? Of course."

Bryan kissed his wife. "I'm on it."

Sheralyn had to go sit with her kids and Gina decided to find her mother. She passed by a row of seniors reclining like reigning queens in the deck chairs along the length of the pool. Red-checkered cloths covered the tables. A cool breeze lifted her hair and she heard sounds from the dance floor as a bow brushed across a fiddle's strings.

She stopped often, speaking to family members of the Garden Club that she hadn't seen in years. It was beginning to get dark but she finally saw her mother at a large round table on the edge of the lawn. She was deep in discussion with Grace.

"Do you remember, Grace?" she heard her mother saying as she sat down. "That summer when you and I decided to go for a swim in the stock pond even though our parents told us not to?"

Grace nodded as she stared at her plate.

"We swam around and then I saw a cottonmouth and we practically flew out of there. I've never moved so fast in my life."

This time Grace chuckled. The memory was still there. It was a small victory and Claire smiled broadly until she saw the look on Gina's face.

"What's wrong, Gina?"

"I wanted to tell you," Gina said, clearing her throat, "I didn't get the promotion. At least they made a decision."

Her mother touched her hand. "Oh, honey, I'm so sorry."

"It's okay. I didn't get it. That's it. I wasn't the right person for the job."

"Did they say why?"

"Not enough experience. The Captain said I did great undercover work. At least he thinks I'm qualified, but they had to choose and the others had more experience."

"I'm so sorry," Claire said, her dark blue eyes resting on her daughter.

"Thanks."

"Are you alright?"

"I'll be fine. I just need a little time to get used to the idea."

"I know you'll get it someday, Gina. You will. It's just a matter of time. If that's what you really want."

Gina looked her in the eye. "It is."

"Then there's not a doubt in my mind," said her mother.

Gina believed her. She leaned over and wrapped her arms around her. "Thanks."

Looking over the crowd, Gina saw that the band members were moving onto the dance floor and suddenly she felt the need to find Blake.

"Gina, wait," her mother stopped her. "I want you to know you can say 'no'."

"What do you mean?"

"I want you to know that you don't have to say yes to make me happy. I make a lot of suggestions. But what you do is up to you. I can't help wanting to give you the opportunity but it's your life, not mine."

Gina sat back down. "So if I never come to another Garden Club thing, that's okay?"

"Well, that sort of hurts. But, even if I don't like it, I'll know that's your decision. But, please, promise me we'll try to find something to do together? It doesn't have to be about flowers."

Gina felt her eyes begin to water. It was if they'd crossed a great divide. Her mother had put that thing into words that neither of them had known even existed until that moment. She wanted Gina to be Gina. And then they set another record, two hugs in one night, until one of the band members took hold of the microphone.

"Hello, how is everyone on this beautiful Texas evening?" The crowd cheered. "That's good," he shouted over the noise. "We thought we'd start off the evening with a good old two-step. How does that sound for all you kicker dancers out there?"

Across the crowd, Mona launched from a chair and waved for Cleeve to meet her on the dance floor. He pretended to protest, reluctantly handing off his Corona to someone, but then hurried to her. They took hold of one another and the music started with a scream of violin strings as Cleeve twirled her, beaming like a teenager, guiding her forward in a perfect way that could only be explained by hundreds of dances before.

Gina gave her mother's hand a quick squeeze as Bryan parted the crowd, pulling Sheralyn behind him. It was their turn to launch into a polka that took them in circles around his parents. Father and son laughed across the floor at each other, challenging to see who could go faster. Gradually more couples went out on to the dance floor and then suddenly Gina was in Blake's arms, holding on for dear life. He held her tightly, dancing for both of them.

He never hesitated. It took everything she had to concentrate on her feet and when she looked up she caught him looking at her, then he pressed his hand into the small of her back to keep her with him. The first dance ended but he didn't let go. The next one started and his hand gripped hers while his arm draped over her shoulders like a real cowboy, and then he threw back his head and laughed. She knew that all she had to do was hold on. He would take care of the rest.

Their faces were wet with sweat when the band finally took a break. They filled their plates with ribs and potato salad then sat at a long picnic table with the others, eating the tender meat with their fingers while the dark red bar-b-que sauce ran down their chins.

"Where'd you learn to dance like that?" Bryan asked Blake, licking sauce from his fingers.

"Hey, I'm a boy from Fort Worth. I was in some cowboy bar almost every Friday night when I was in high school. You were pretty impressive, too," he said, elbowing Gina.

A loud howling erupted from the direction of the barn. The voices grew louder until one of the husbands appeared in the darkness, dragging a protesting teenager by his forearm. The boy's mother stormed barefooted across the grass to meet them and their voices drifted up to the audience, enough for most of them to know it had something to do with drinking and being fourteen.

"Things never change, do they?" said Brooke to Gina.

"Listen, Blake," Bryan began, "I know this is last minute, but do you want to go hunting tomorrow? Dad and I are going to our place in West Texas. "

"I'd love it. I haven't been hunting in years so I may embarrass myself."

"I doubt it. Dad and I are terrible shots, but who cares? I've got an extra gun if you need it."

"I've got one. What time?"

Gina listened as the men made their plans. She couldn't believe how well things were going.

Eventually, the older generation yielded to their need for sleep and said their goodbyes. The grandchildren were happily entertaining themselves and their parents were free to actually relax. Voices carried by the night air talked of old memories and remembrances of Garden Club traditions as couples stood in small groups, scattered across the lawn. Every few minutes, the sound of laughter floated in the air and then sharper tones mixed with love as little ones were told they had *just one more minute* in the pool before being lifted out by an arm, wrapped in a towel, and told to sit in one place until they dried off.

Gina and Blake found two empty lounge chairs, the same ones the mothers had relinquished, and watched the winding down of the evening. They listened to the noises of the fathers and mothers, shouts of kids chasing each other in the dark, a cow lowing somewhere far away. Blake let his arm drop between them and then Gina lowered hers. Their fingers wound together. His skin was tight and rough as he moved a finger up and down one of hers. Her heart began to race. They looked at one another and smiled.

Gina looked across the pool and saw Cleeve and Bryan lounging in an identical pair of chairs, talking quietly. Bryan's youngest son was curled up in his father's lap, lulled asleep by the sound of his father's voice and the feel of a hand gently stroking his head.

Gina knew it would never be much better than this.

CHAPTER 32

At first they drove in silence.

"Cleeve asked me to do a painting of the ranch. One with the sun setting."

"Really? That would be so cool."

Silence again.

"I'm getting on a private plane in the morning."

"I know."

"I must have passed the test."

They were both smiling in the darkness.

"I wasn't worried about the guys," said Gina. "It's the mothers you need to worry about."

"I think they liked me.

"I don't know. You were a little crazy out there on the dance floor. Either way, I'm sure I'll be hearing about it." She reached over and put her hand on his shoulder. "Thank you."

"For what?"

"For being okay with all that."

"It was fun. But is it okay if our next date does not include your mother? Or any of the mothers?"

"Please, yes!"

Blake was looking at her and his voice was soft and deep. "Do you think you could scoot over and sit a little closer?" He didn't have to ask again.

Forty-five minutes later, they stood in the hallway outside her door, her back pressed against the dark wood.

"Would you like to come in?"

His fingers brushed her hair from her face, his eyes locked on hers. Time seemed to stop. She had never felt so completely safe, so unbelievably calm with someone she still barely knew. She asked him again with her eyes.

"I'd better not. Early morning," he answered slowly, running a finger down her arm, then back up, as though it were a brush stroke.

He did it again, this time on the other arm. Gently, she pushed his arms away, trying to focus. "That's right. You better not be late. Cleeve and Bryan won't wait. If they said six a.m., they'll probably be in the air by 6:05."

Reluctantly, he took a step back. "Good to know."

"What will you do if you actually shoot something?"

"I have absolutely no idea. It never crossed my mind." Suddenly, he leaned down to her and brushed her lips with his, then pressed in and kissed her mouth, taking her upper lip, then the lower one, then back again. He stopped, frozen, and stared into her eyes, then straightened up. Gina gasped for air.

"Goodnight," he said softly, backing down the hall. Gina blinked and nodded. She attempted to wave.

"Next time, no mothers. Got it?"

"Got it," she mumbled, then turned and unlocked her door.

"Have fun working on your flower arrangement," she heard him say as she closed the door behind her.

Gina slipped to the floor against the door. "I will."

Bad Guy sauntered out of the bedroom and parked himself in front of her, licking a paw. The cat squealed when Gina swept him up and buried her face in his fur.

After showering and crawling into bed, Gina thought about how wonderful everything seemed to be. Unless duty called, the whole weekend was hers and the first thing on her list was something she'd been thinking about for a long time. She was going to buy a car.

It had been four years since she'd owned her own car. After joining the force, it hadn't been necessary because they wanted her to use the cars from the pool, but now she wanted her own. She was tired of feeling like she needed a vaccination at the end of every day.

Saturday morning, Gina bought a black SUV. It was big and powerful, and she'd already arranged it with the Captain to install the latest gadgets. It was his way of saying he felt bad she didn't get the promotion. That evening, with her new car sitting in the underground garage, Gina got out her organizer and planned her week. She and the others were going to do their best, for themselves and the mothers.

Gina made a note to order her flowers on Monday. Wednesday, containers needed to be chosen. Flowers needed to be picked up on Thursday, and on Friday, the day before the big show (there was a large red X across it on her calendar), was the day to create the best arrangements possible. The mothers and daughters had already discussed times and places to work on them together. Everyone was expected to do at least two arrangements.

Gina wrote in one more reminder. Bad Guy needed to be checked into the kitty hotel for a four day stay. Then she'd be ready for the flower show.

CHAPTER 33

Monday morning, Claire woke early and was having her coffee when the phone rang. She hoped it might be Gina to talk about her date with Blake, but it wasn't Gina. It was SueBee, and suddenly she felt as if someone had sunk an ice cold blade into her heart.

"No! No! No!" she kept saying, over and over again, until she finally stopped and SueBee told her the rest of what had happened.

Claire hung up and bowed her head over the phone, praying for the strength to pick it up again. Her hands shook as she dialed Gina's number.

"Gina!" She gasped a giant sob, then covered her mouth, not wanting to lose control but at the sound of Gina's voice it was more than she could bear.

"What is it, Mom?"

"Are you at home?"

"No, I'm at the coffee shop with Helen and Brooke. We're still waiting on Sheralyn." Then Claire remembered the girls had planned on meeting early to make a few last minute arrangements for that Saturday. Lately, they'd been together almost every day.

At the mention of Sheralyn's name, Claire forced herself to be quiet. She had to. She pressed her forehead into her hand.

"What is it, Mom? What's wrong?" Gina begged.

"Cleeve and Bryan are gone." It was like poison coming out of her mouth. The words made it real and she had to force herself to go on.

"The plane crashed. They were coming home from the hunting trip and had an accident. They're dead. It's so horrible." Her voice cracked.

"What? What are you talking about? Are you sure? That can't be true." Gina's voice suddenly dropped to whisper one more word. "Blake?"

"I don't know. They told Mona they had trouble identifying the bodies. Have you heard from him?"

"No." Gina's voice was muffled and Claire knew she must be talking to the others. Finally she came back on and Claire realized it wasn't Gina her daughter, it was Gina the police officer.

"Where is everyone? Should I come get you? Should I make any calls? Where do you need me?"

"No, no, we've done all that. I'm still home but as soon as I can get dressed, I'm going over to Mona's. SueBee is already there and the others will be there soon. ."

"Is Sheralyn there?"

"I'm sure she is. Her parents are driving over from Arkansas and they should be here by this afternoon."

"We'll get there as soon as we can," said Gina.

"Hurry," whispered Claire.

Claire recognized most of the cars that were already parked outside Mona's house when she arrived a few minutes later. She let herself in through the kitchen door and immediately saw Ginger on the phone. There were others, sitting at the kitchen table drinking coffee or organizing the food that was already starting to pile up.

Ruby's strong body leaned against the sink. At the sound of the door, she looked up and, seeing it was Claire, came at her with dripping hands. Cleeve and Bryan were family. As Claire pressed her face into Ruby's shoulder, she pictured the wink in Cleeve's eye and the way he loved to tease anyone and everyone, especially Mona. Reluctantly they separated. Claire wanted to find Mona.

According to SueBee, the three men had taken off on Sunday afternoon as planned, but something had happened and Cleeve had turned the private plane back to the little airport outside of Lubbock. Then Cleeve had called Mona to tell her it was a small thing, that they'd be late and she shouldn't wait up. Sheralyn got the same message from Bryan, and that was the last thing they'd heard until the Lubbock Police Department called Mona early that morning. She'd called SueBee first, probably because she knew SueBee was an early riser.

Claire paused at the top of the stairs to catch her breath. The house felt like a morgue, as though it were in mourning with them. She hadn't been upstairs in Mona's house since she'd had surgery a few years ago. The walls were a museum white and decorated with expensive art work. The hall was lined with a thick runner that swallowed her footsteps. She gripped the knob on Mona's bedroom door, hesitated, then let herself inside.

The master suite was enormous. There was a sitting area with wide doorways into a dressing room, and beyond that was a bathroom almost as big as Claire's bedroom at home. Someone had drawn the drapes but there was still a sliver of hot Texas sun so the room was not completely dark.

Mona and Sheralyn held each other in the middle of the king-sized bed, their legs covered with a light blanket. SueBee and Charlotte were on the edges of the bed. The phone rang angrily before it was answered by someone from Garden Club who spoke into the receiver softly, then set it silently back in its cradle.

Sheralyn pressed her face into Mona's shoulder, "I told Bryan not to let Cleeve keep him too late." Charlotte began rubbing her back. "I'll never see him again, and the boys, those poor babies." Her sobs took over and Claire heard several of the others sniffing.

Mona raised her face, speaking softly to the ceiling. "Cleeve, please come home, I need you to come home."

Claire hurried to the bed, crowding next to SueBee so that she could take Mona's hand.

"I'm here, honey, I'm here."

"Oh, Claire," Mona said, "he called me after lunch, right after I saw you at church, and he was so happy. Did I tell you they'd met some Dallas people? That man could not go anywhere in the world without meeting somebody to make friends with." She wearily pulled back her hand and rubbed Sheralyn's back. "He promised he would leave before dark, but you know Cleeve – he has never cared about time. Then the plane..." Her voice broke. "I wish he hadn't flown in the dark. Poor thing."

Mona gulped suddenly, as if she'd suddenly remembered again that he was gone.

The bedroom door opened and Gina, Brooke, and Helen stood in the doorway. Charlotte immediately moved so that Brooke could take her place at Sheralyn's back.

"We're here, Sheralyn," Brooke said softly. "I'm so sorry, so so sorry."

It was Sheralyn's turn to raise her head at the sound of her friend's voice. There were brown moons beneath her eyes and her cheekbones looked like carved stone. Gina leaned in to kiss her cheek.

From the sounds outside the door, it was obvious the news of the accident had spread. The front door bell rang every few minutes and there was the sound of strange voices. Claire knew she'd stay for just a little longer before going back down. There were enough members to stay with Mona and she felt she'd be of better use in the kitchen where enough food to last a week was expected. Flower arrangements were also arriving and she needed to make sure someone was taking care of them since they'd be needed for the funeral. No one had mentioned the funerals yet. That would come later.

As the day passed, the sun rose higher in the sky until only a few rays streaked across the kitchen sink, filling the room with a deep shade of afternoon gold. The backyard was half in shadows and Claire wondered if she should go back upstairs and make Mona come sit with her outside in one of the rocking chairs on the back porch. But she knew she wouldn't come. Had it only been a month since they'd been sitting there together, waiting to judge their last flower show? Cleeve had looked so handsome.

Claire sent tempting plates of food upstairs, but each time they came back untouched. It was almost two when Sheralyn finally appeared in the doorway, Gina and Brooke on either side of her, helping her to the table. Claire immediately put a small platter of finger sandwiches in front them and made sure a box of tissues sat close by.

Gingerly, Sheralyn picked up a sandwich and held it between her fingertips. She looked at it, then touched it to her lips. Poor thing, Claire thought, the girl looks like she's been emptied of all emotion.

"How are the children?" Helen asked from the desk where she'd been taking her turn at answering the phone. She'd already told the story over and over.

"I know, it's so sad, the plane went down outside of Lubbock. Yes, they have two little boys, they are so precious. Sheralyn and Mona are overwhelmed right now, but we aren't leaving their sides. No, I think we have plenty of food. No, no plans have been made. It will be in the paper soon. Okay, I've written down your name, I'll tell them you called. Thank you. Yes, thank you for calling."

Silently, Claire prayed for the phone not to ring, at least for the next few minutes.

"They're with friends," Sheralyn answered. "I haven't told them yet. How do you tell a child they'll never see their father again?" She closed her eyes and a tear traced its way down her cheek. Gina touched it with a tissue.

"How about a brownie," Claire suggested. She set down a plate of lemon squares and brownies. She couldn't help but think how beautiful Sheralyn was, though in a haunting way, as she roused herself enough to take a small bite of the sandwich.

Claire motioned for Gina to meet her by the sink.

"Anything about Blake?"

"No," said Gina, "and I don't know what to do. I can't leave Sheralyn. I've called the Sheriff's department and they're looking into it. The wreckage is still being investigated. I can't stand this, Mom. I don't know what to do."

Claire hugged her tight. "We keep praying. God knows."

SueBee walked in and kept going toward the back door. She motioned for the others to follow. Helen stayed with Sheralyn.

"Ginger is going to stay the night with Mona. Can either of you stay with Sheralyn?" she asked. Brooke and Gina both raised a hand. "Good. When Sheralyn's ready, see if you can get her to tell you what you can do for her at her house. Do we need to go feed animals? Is there a security system? At least until her mother gets here." Both nodded.

The phone rang inside and they heard Helen's voice answering before shouting, "Gina!"

Gina hurried back in. Helen held out the phone, shaking it at her.

"Hello?" Gina said, before collapsing into a chair and doubled over, the phone still pressed against her ear.

"Blake?"

CHAPTER 34

Gina's legs were draped across Blake's lap as she lay huddled in his arms on the couch in Mona's living room. Her head rested against his chest and she could feel the steady beat of his heart. They were both exhausted and Gina felt her eyelids grow heavy as she fought to keep them open. Her breathing slowed, her thoughts finally settling now that she knew he was safe.

Blake was exhausted, too. He'd been driving all night, then heard the news from Gina and raced to get there for Mona and Sheralyn. He'd spent the last hour in the room alone with them.

When Gina had first heard his voice, she'd started to cry and then realized he had no idea what had happened. As soon as she told him, Blake was out the door and on his way over.

"He's alive," Sheralyn echoed gently when Gina had put down the phone. She wanted Gina to take her hand.

"Yes," Gina said.

"That's wonderful. Will you please ask him to come up and see me when he gets here?"

Gina nodded, then Sheralyn soundlessly raised herself up from the table and left the room. Brooke went with her.

"They wanted to know everything," Blake said, stroking Gina's hair. "They made me start from the minute we left Dallas until the minute I watched them lift off in the plane to come home. They wanted to hear every single thing we talked about, what we laughed about. What we had for breakfast. I even told them how Cleeve and Bryan almost made me sick talking about them. It was constant, and always about how much they loved them. I was jealous, you know? They both had something special with their wives."

The house seemed to be at peace with itself. There was only the occasional phone ringing or muffled voice coming from the kitchen. It was dark outside and Gina tried to rouse herself, afraid she would fall asleep and never wake up. Blake needed to leave, then she'd find something from the kitchen to eat before going upstairs to see if Sheralyn needed her.

Blake shifted her in his arms. She knew he needed her as much as she needed him.

"Bryan got a deer," he said, "and then we realized we had the perfect solution to get it home. Those guys we met from Dallas had a truck and Cleeve talked them into letting me go with them to drive it back. It was all a big joke. I got to be the one to 'chaperone' the deer. When I tried calling the house this morning, it was to tell Cleeve that Bryan's deer was at the taxidermy's place in Denton."

Gina breathed in deeply. He still smelled of sweat and coffee. Later, as she kissed him goodnight at the door, he lifted her face and told her he thought she was beautiful and then he kissed her tenderly on the mouth.

Twenty-four hours later, there wasn't very much for the daughters to do. The mothers had written the obituaries and delivered the details for the program to the printer. They'd made appointments for Mona and Sheralyn to meet with the minister and the funeral home. The daughters were asked to be available to help with the reception on Saturday but of course they didn't have to ask.

The three of them, Brooke, Helen and Gina, ended up in Mona's living room with their shoes off and their feet up on the coffee table. They wanted to have a quiet moment together before everyone needed to go back to their own lives. Brooke poured three glasses of wine, then rose to take a tour of Mona's bookcases. She walked slowly, reading the titles of the leather-bound books with one arm draped across her belly while the other held her glass. Gina thought how much she resembled her mother. Suddenly, Brooke whirled around to face them. She was holding one of the mini-trophies.

"Oh my gosh ya'll, what about the Excelsior?"

There was a collective gasp. It had been completely forgotten.

"It's this Saturday!"

"I can't believe we forgot about it," Gina said. "I was supposed to order my flowers yesterday."

"Wait," said Helen, "what are we saying? We can't do the flower show. Not without the mothers and I doubt they're going to have anything to do with it."

Gina felt relieved and then she felt guilty for it. "You're right, there's no way we can win without them and that was the whole point, right?"

The weight on her foot shifted and she leaned down to rub the old dog's belly. He was waiting for his master but she'd have to do. Rubbing him made them both feel better.

Brooke offered, "Then should we say anything? I wonder if they've forgotten, too."

"Probably," said Helen, "but you can never tell with the mothers."

"Okay, I'll go ask," Gina said.

She found her mother at the kitchen desk.

"What are you doing, Mom?"

"I'm making out a schedule for tomorrow."

Gina leaned over her shoulder and looked at her mother's perfect handwriting. She'd spent hours trying to copy it as a child, tracing the letters slowly with big fat pencils.

"I've been trying to get Mona to help me make some of the decisions," her mother said, "but I haven't made much progress. The bodies will be at the funeral home tomorrow. I think we're going to plan on having the graveside and funeral on Saturday."

"That's what I wanted to talk to you about," said Gina.

"You look tired, Gina."

"I'm taking this week off, Mom, I'm fine, but we need to..."

"Really? Well good for you. And don't think we haven't noticed how you girls have taken care of Sheralyn. Thank you."

"Of course." Gina sat against the desk to face her. "Mom, we completely forgot about the flower show. It's this Saturday, remember? So no flower show, right?"

Her mother's eyes opened slightly wider, a sign she'd forgotten, too, but her expression didn't change. "All that work gone to waste," she said. "I don't see how we can possibly even think about that now."

"Who should I call to tell them we're dropping out?"

"You will not drop out of the flower show!"

Gina and her mother both jumped.

"You may *not* drop out of the flower show," Mona repeated from behind them, "and you still have to win. Do not quit. I don't care what you have to do, even without our entries or Sheralyn's entries. Got it? I don't care if you have to cheat."

Without her dark glasses or make-up, she looked fragile, even with Charlotte and SueBee standing on either side of her, holding her up. She was slightly stooped from the exhaustion of coming downstairs. But her eyes were like fireballs and her jaw was set.

"But Mona," Gina said, "we can't win without you. And we want to be at the funeral. That's much more important than the flower show."

"Gina, you and I have disagreed on a lot of things, but I am asking you to do this for me. Please don't give up. That would not be honoring to Cleeve or to Bryan."

She didn't wait for Gina to answer and pointed a trembling hand toward the door. Charlotte and SueBee tenderly moved her in that direction.

"I guess we aren't dropping out," Gina said when they were gone.

"I guess not," answered her mother.

CHAPTER 35

By Friday afternoon, the mothers and daughters had done their jobs well. The mothers had made sure all the arrangements were ready for the funeral and reception and the girls had completed at least three arrangements each for the flower show. Still, Gina had one more favor to ask of her mother and found her where she'd been all week, working in Mona's kitchen.

"Mom, do you think a few of the moms could come by the Exhibit Hall early tomorrow morning to look at the arrangements? We'd really like your opinion, see if we need to do any last minute touch-ups. It will only take a few minutes."

"Tomorrow morning?"

Gina nodded.

"But the funeral is tomorrow."

"I know, but it's at eleven. We just need you a little before nine."

"Oh no, honey, the graveside's at nine, then the memorial is at ten. We're expecting everyone back at Mona's around eleven. I'll be at Mona's beginning at seven-thirty. There's just too much to coordinate."

Gina wasn't surprised, but she was very disappointed. They'd all worked like crazy, attacking the flower show as if it were the most important thing in the world. They'd even gone all over town to find the best flowers, critiqued each other's ideas, scoured flea markets for the perfect containers, and worked for hours on their arrangements. They hoped they were ready but not until they had the mothers' blessing would they feel they'd done their best.

"Okay. I just hope we can make it to the church in time for the funeral," said Gina.

"Oh, I hope so," said her mother. "I would hate for you to have to walk in late."

CHAPTER 36

Saturday turned out to be a beautiful day for a funeral. Claire rose earlier than usual and took a long bath. She'd gotten her hair done the day before and felt good in the black suit she reserved for funerals.

She pulled her car around back and parked in front of Mona's garage. SueBee's Buick pulled in right behind her and they walked in together. Others arrived, quietly taking direction on what needed to be done and who was needed where. Ruby and Richard slipped into their routine of unwrapping dishes and setting out chairs while tables started going up outside. The dining room table was laid out with the Club's silver, slowly being filled with cakes and pies that had been taking up space in the butler's pantry. SueBee was soon cutting and dusting the lemon squares with powdered sugar while Charlotte, assuming Mona's usual job, draped a damp towel over the finger sandwiches to keep them moist.

Cleeve had served on several boards, some for over twenty years. He'd also been on the city council, a deacon at the church and president of the Salesmanship Club. So it was no wonder that dozens of flower arrangements had arrived to honor him. Claire walked between the rooms, looking at the wreaths and sprays. The Garden Club had struggled to decide how they should best be displayed, but they'd found the perfect spot for each one.

As they'd gotten closer to Saturday, Mona and Sheralyn had made it very clear that they wanted the caskets covered with flowers and made it Claire's job to choose the perfect dozen. When things were humming in the kitchen, she'd decided on which ones and marked them with a white tissue tucked between the blooms. They were moved into the entry hall in time for the nine o'clock pick up.

The doorbell rang.

"That must be the funeral home," Claire said to Ruby. She looked at her watch, "And they're early. It's only 8:45." She put down the strawberries she'd been cutting and wiped her hands on her apron and hurried to let them in.

As she walked to the door, she ran over the schedule one more time in her head. The family had already left for the private graveside, she and the others would leave for the church around nine-thirty for the ten o'clock service with everything ready back at the house for the reception.

"We want you to take the long way, use Lakeside or Fairway," Claire said to the two men eyeing the arrangements. "They have less turns and you can go slower. We've already added water and some of it will spill but that's alright. We just don't want them falling over. And some of these sprays might need someone to hold them. Is there anyone who can do that?"

"We have box frames in the van, ma'am," the driver said. "Don't worry, we've done this a bunch of times before. Nothing's going to happen to them."

"And when you get to the church, please divide them up evenly between the caskets. Don't put all the sprays on one side and the bouquets on the other. See how some are red, some are purple?"

"Yes, Ma'am."

"Split them up. Put some red on each side, some purple. I think that big white one with the roses and peonies should go in the center. What do you think?" The man seemed to know she really didn't care what he thought.

"It was a gift from Mr. Johnson's old bank board and we all think it should take center stage."

"Well, all right," said Claire, once they were done loading. "Be careful. We are a garden club you know. The flowers are more important to us than probably any funeral you've ever done."

They didn't answer and she watched as they drove away, wincing when they turned the corner. "I'm sure I'm going to have to rearrange them once I get there," she said out loud, then turned to go back inside.

CHAPTER 37

Gina raced around the condo, grabbing her shoes, running back in the bathroom to get her earrings, back to the kitchen then back to her closet to get a sweater. She was dressed for the funeral, but had the flowers to get to the convention center. They had all agreed to try and get the arrangements there by nine, then they'd have thirty minutes to do touch-ups and still get to the church in plenty of time for the service.

At eight-thirty, Gina stepped back and gave her three arrangements one last look. She felt like they actually might have a chance.

Just as she'd done before the last flower show, Gina drove slowly and carefully up through the underground parking garage. But this time, the arrangements were securely lodged in the wood frame Blake had built in the back of the SUV. Also different, when she pulled onto the street, there was only sunshine and clear skies. It was going to be the perfect day for a flower show.

Gina navigated the one way streets and freeways to get across town to the Convention Center. It was not far, just complicated. She watched the flowers in her rear-view mirror but felt herself begin to relax. They couldn't move an inch in the wood frames.

The Escalade still smelled of new leather as she ran her fingers around the steering wheel, admiring her purchase. At the next red light, out of habit she turned on her police scanner. A homeless man knocked on her window, making her jump, but she showed him her badge and he quickly folded up his sign and shuffled across the street.

Suddenly, the radio crackled to life. "Unit 261, please be advised, two-vehicle possible injury accident at Weston and Charles. Ambulance has been called."

Gina was on Weston now and she recognized the intersection right away. Between Downtown and the Convention Center was a wide swath of open land that had been a river a century ago. Usually it was dry, but during heavy rains, it filled with water and people resurrected their flat bottomed boats and canoes. A levee had been built to span the divide and Weston Road sat on top of it. It was like a giant moat spanned by a rib with monstrous green sloping shoulders.

Weston Road had always been accident prone. People thought they could pass along the narrow ribbon of road, but the shoulders were slippery and if anyone strayed even slightly, they typically overcorrected and off they'd go, down the side of the embankment. Most of the time they landed right side up, but sometimes they rolled and people got hurt.

Gina gave the arrangements a quick glance, then sped up. The accident was easy to spot. A large white van was cab end down in the ditch and a small white Mercedes dangled above it. It looked as though the car had driven right off the road and directly onto the van.

Gina pulled her SUV along the dirt shoulder and turned on her lights. She began making her way down the muddy incline before realizing her high heeled shoes were all wrong and tossed them back up to the car. Her eye caught movement in the Mercedes, but she was more worried about the people in the van and hurried to the smashed cab. The door dangled open and a man's body was slumped into the wheel.

"Are you okay?" Gina asked the driver. Empty chip bags and water bottles filled the space above the dash. He seemed to be dazed and was taking off his seatbelt. There was another passenger who had already gotten out on the other side and was sitting on the ground, holding his head. A small trickle of blood ran down his arm.

The driver rolled out. The airbag had gone off and white powder covered his face.

"I think so," he said. "My partner is a little shook up. I already called an ambulance."

Gina took a few steps back, craning her neck to see the driver of the Mercedes. It was solidly stuck on top of the van. A woman's face appeared in the window. Smiling down at Gina was Brooke.

"Hi, Gina, is everyone okay?"

"Brooke? What in the heck are you doing up there? Are you okay?"

"I'm fine. I was trying to pass this guy and he started to swerve out and it made me hit the gravel. Then I spun around a few times and somehow, I ended up here. I'm stuck."

"Are your arrangements in there?"

Brooke looked over her shoulder and started laughing.

"They're fine. Now if I can just climb down out of here."

Gina heard sirens in the distance.

"A fire truck will be here soon. Are you sure you're okay?"

"I'm good. But what are we going to do? We've got to get to the show."

"Can you hand them down to me?"

Carefully, Brooke flipped over and one at a time, handed down her three arrangements to Gina who then walked them up the hill. She was grateful Blake had built out the whole space so she could easily fit them into the extra compartments. At the same time, the fire truck and ambulance arrived and helped Brooke down. The police took Brooke's information, and Gina got permission for both of them to leave. Gina tried cleaning herself off before putting her shoes back on.

"Gina, you've got to come look at this," Brooke called from below.

"We've got to go. Come on."

"No, Gina, you really need to come see this."

Gina growled in frustration and went back down the grassy incline. She followed Brooke's direction and looked over the seats and into the back of the van. It was like a bomb had gone off at a greenhouse. There were destroyed flowers and upside down vases everywhere.

"Look," Brooke said, pointing toward one. It was a large white arrangement of roses and peonies. Gina's heart sank. They were looking at the flowers from Mona's house. The one with roses and peonies had been her mother's favorite. It was the one meant for the center table at the memorial service.

Gina looked at Brooke.

"What are we going to do?"

CHAPTER 38

Charlotte and SueBee rode with Claire and were relieved to get the last handicapped spot. Inside, the organ was already playing a familiar hymn.

They walked single file down the center aisle to the third row and moved a *Reserved* sign so they could slide into the pew. The rest of Garden Club gradually arrived, filling the row. The front two pews were still vacant, waiting for the family. The organist finished one hymn and began another. It was still early.

"It's too bad the girls can't sit up here close to Sheralyn," SueBee whispered to Claire.

"I know. They'll just have to sit in the back. I'm sure Sheralyn understands."

Claire stared at the two large mahogany caskets, centered on the stage. There was a tall easel between them that held a blown up photograph of Bryan and Cleeve, grinning for the camera. It was obvious they were father and son.

Claire leaned over to SueBee.

"You know, I usually sit on the piano side of the church when I come to funerals, it seems so strange sitting on the organ side." Suddenly, her eyes darted to the caskets.

"Where are the flowers?" Claire asked, grabbing SueBee's arm.

"That's strange. I thought they would have gotten here before us."

Claire leaned over SueBee and whispered down the row, "Does anyone know where the flowers are? Why aren't they here?" No one knew.

Claire looked at the back of the church where the funeral people were standing. They weren't doing anything but greeting people and handing out programs. She got up and walked back there.

"Excuse me, but where are the flowers? Those caskets are supposed to be covered in flowers. Your people picked them up from the house thirty minutes ago."

The two men dressed in dark grey suits were just as surprised. They looked down front then over the heads of the filling pews as if the flowers could possibly be anywhere else but on stage. "I don't know," said the taller of the two. "Let me go make a call."

Claire hurried back down the aisle to her seat.

"They're making a call. They have no idea. I don't think they even noticed. Can you believe that?"

SueBee shook her head. By now the other ladies knew and their heads were swiveling around every few seconds in hopes of seeing someone coming down the aisle with the arrangements.

Claire felt her blood pressure rising. All those gorgeous arrangements! What would Mona think when she saw her husband's and son's caskets naked like that. She wondered if she might find arrangements scattered in other parts of the church when suddenly, there was a loud downbeat on the organ.

The minister came through a door at the right and walked solemnly to the stage. At the podium, he lifted his arms for the audience to stand. The organist began playing "Great is Thy Faithfulness" and then the family began filing in, led by Mona and followed by her two brothers. Sheralyn came in next, holding her children's hands.

The Garden Club stared at Mona, following her every step. The dark glasses made her look Audrey-esque and she wore a small pillbox hat with black netting that covered her face. Mona suddenly froze as she looked directly at her husband's and son's bare caskets. Her shoulders sagged and she gripped her brother's arm, until finally she let him lead her to the first pew where she sat, facing her men.

Claire gripped SueBee's arm. There were tears in her eyes, in all their eyes.

"You may be seated," the minister began. "On behalf of the family, I want to thank you..." and then he stopped, staring at the back of the church. Claire followed his gaze as everyone turned to look.

A beautiful arrangement of red roses appeared to be floating down the aisle. Behind it was another spray of flowers, this one of magnolia blossoms and behind that were ten more arrangements, hibiscus and Lily of the Valley, all looking more beautiful than any arrangement she'd ever seen.

Chills ran down her body. As the arrangements got closer, Claire recognized her daughter's delicate hands wrapped around the first vase and despite the hushed silence in the church, she wanted to stand up and cheer. She could hardly believe how perfect each one looked, and from the sounds from the crowd, no one else could either. Gina passed by and looked at her. She'd never been so proud of anything in her life.

Gina and Brooke solemnly placed the arrangements around the caskets, then squeezed into the pew next to their mothers.

"Let us pray," said the minister. "Our Father, who art in Heaven, hallowed be Thy name..."

Claire looked up and caught her daughter's eye.

CHAPTER 39

After the funeral, a young girl carrying a piece of lemon pound cake wound her way around white linen tablecloths and folding chairs until she got to the last table before the swimming pool. Claire accepted the cake.

"Thank you, Mary Lee. How's your mother doing?"

"She's fine."

"Do they need any help in the kitchen?" asked SueBee, sitting next to Claire.

"I don't think so. It's pretty crowded in there."

"Tell her to come outside when she can. We want to visit with her. And you might want to pick up a few of those dirty plates on that table over there on your way back in. Might as well make use of those strong arms."

"Yes, Mrs. Sessions."

Claire watched Brooke's oldest daughter do as she was told. Grace watched her, too, a confused look on her face.

"Is that Randall's daughter?"

"No, it's Charlotte's granddaughter. Isn't she a cutie?"

"She sure is," said Grace softly. "I think Randall's dead, anyway."

"Probably so," said Claire. "Oh look, here come the girls."

Gina took the empty chair Claire had saved for her as Brooke and Helen pulled up chairs. Gina's hair was in a French twist and she let Claire lift up a strand that had fallen out.

"We just got the results from the others still at the convention center," Gina announced to the mothers. "We didn't win the Excelsior."

"Oh darn," said Claire.

"Oh, that's okay. We weren't expecting to win anyway, but I just heard something that makes everything worth it." Gina was grinning from ear to ear.

"What?" asked Claire.

"The Goldenrods got arrested."

"For what?" asked Claire.

"I told you they cheated," said SueBee.

"They weren't cheating, at least that's not the point," said Gina. "After Brooke and I found the wrecked arrangements, we called the others to make sure it was okay with them. We knew we couldn't win without them but we all agreed the funeral was more important. But right after the service, Brooke and I went back to see how the others had done, and..."

"And?" said Charlotte anxiously.

"Just as they were about to announce the winner, in walked the cops and they got arrested for burglary."

"They're burglars?" said Claire.

"Just a few of them, but they were the ones behind that burglary ring I've been working for a year. Rich girls who got a thrill out of stealing. They used the garden club to get to know wealthy women, and then they would ask them to join but really they were finding out about their security system, when the help was there, things like that. Once they figured out the family's schedule, they were in and out. They never sold anything because they weren't doing it for the money – it was a game to them."

"This is a whole lot better than getting caught for cheating," SueBee concluded. "Congratulations, Gina."

"Did you get credit for that, honey?" Claire asked.

"Maybe a little bit, but I had no idea it would happen today. I also told the Captain about my suspicions about The Village."

Their smiles vanished.

Gina smiled. "Don't worry, I told him that my informant discovered that the supplier had decided to move his operation to Colorado, because it's legal in Colorado, of course. I checked with some independent businessmen, whose last name just happens to be Barrister, and it turned out they were in the middle of getting their license to open up shop. They actually liked the idea of carrying on the family business and want to continue in the spirit of their mother's intentions which is to help those who really need it in their declining years. Legally, of course."

"That's wonderful, Gina," said SueBee.

"Does that mean we are out of the business?" asked Charlotte.

"I'm afraid so. The boys are planning on clearing out the closets this week. No questions asked."

"I guess it was a good thing after all for them to move to Colorado," said Charlotte.

"And they're keeping you out of jail," said Gina. "I'd say everything worked out very well."

"But what about Claire?" asked Charlotte.

"What do you mean?" asked Gina.

Claire shot Charlotte a look that told her to shut up but Gina saw it.

"Mom?"

"Charlotte knows how much I enjoyed my job keeping the books, that's all," said Claire.

"Well," said Gina, "why do you have to stop? The business is in Colorado, but you can still help with things over the phone. I bet the Barrister boys would love to have someone with your experience."

"And they should pay you, right?" said Charlotte.

Claire let out a deep breath and smiled. "Very nice. Thank you, Gina, for keeping us out of jail."

"Jail?" Mona asked, walking up with Sheralyn. "Is someone going to jail?"

Everyone moved around so that she and Sheralyn could sit. Both were pale and obviously exhausted, but at least they were able to leave the bedroom. That was a start.

"Just the Goldenrods," said Claire, and she explained what had happened.

"Justice is served," said Mona.

"I'm sorry we didn't win for you, Mona," said Gina.

"What you did was perfect. If there hadn't been flowers, I don't know how I would have gotten through the service. And to see your arrangement," she touched Gina's hand and nodded to Brooke, "and yours, meant more than you'll ever know. Sheralyn and I needed to see the flowers, didn't we?" Sheralyn nodded.

Mona gently took off her glasses. There were deep shadows under her eyes but her lips, thin red lines, parted in a faint smile. "And now I suppose you still want the silver. You know we don't give anything away for nothing."

Gina checked with the others before answering. "Well, as a matter of fact, we, the daughters and the daughters-in-law, are hoping that since we've decided to start our own garden club, you might go ahead and give it to us. We still might want to start a few of our own traditions, though."

"I can't believe it," said Claire, "we've lived to see the birth of the Junior Group of the Hillcrest Heights Garden Club."

"Wait a minute, Mom," Gina said, "who said that was our name?"

"Are you crazy?" said SueBee. "What else could you call it?"

"I don't care," said Mona softly. "They can call themselves whatever they want. They will always be the daughters to us."

CHAPTER 40

Blake took Gina's hand as they slipped out of their shoes and walked barefoot across Mona's front lawn. The caterers were loading their vans with steam tables and boxes of glassware while a long truck from Ducky Bob's backed into the driveway and stopped where Richard had left all the folding chairs and tables in tall stacks. The valet service had already left and only a few cars remained, scattered up and down the street. Most of the mothers had gone home. Their job still wasn't over, but at least for now, they felt like it was alright to go home and take a nap. Mona had insisted.

The grass felt cold beneath Gina's feet and she felt stronger having Blake at her side. He seemed to be able to understand more than just what she was saying. He understood what she was feeling. "How do you recover from losing a husband and son? I wonder how long it will take to even be able to feel normal again. If you ever do."

"They were good men," he said. "I'll never forget them." He squeezed her hand hard, not looking at her, and she felt how much he was hurting. "How's Sheralyn and Mona?"

Gina pictured Cleeve and the way he had winked at her when he knew he was interrupting the Club's meeting in the kitchen. They'd always enjoyed their private conspiracy against Mona. Even Sheralyn appreciated the teasing.

"Sheralyn's strong," said Gina. "A lot stronger than she looks. And she has a strong faith, she and Mona both. They're much closer now. I don't know how long it will take but they'll both be alright."

They had reached the edge of the yard and sat down on a small bench beneath a tree. Blake reached for her hand, his painter ones engulfing hers. The fingers were so long and he'd scrubbed his nails. She lifted one and couldn't help but smile when she saw a tiny speck of red paint wedged in his cuticles.

"What are you working on?"

"The landscape of Cleeve's ranch. Helen's husband sent me a picture he took the night of the picnic. I think I'm going to paint two. One for Mona and one for Sheralyn."

He continued. "I can't help but think there must be something for me to do, a reason why God kept me off that plane. If it hadn't been for that deer…"

Gina turned his face toward hers to silence him. The sun was setting, shooting its rays through the trees and almost directly into her eyes so that she could barely make out the outline of his face. She reached up with her arms and circled his neck, and pulled him down to her until their lips came together, and then he kissed her hard. She had to stop him, but only long enough to take a breath and mutter, "Thank God for that deer."

42056090R00123

Made in the USA
San Bernardino, CA
25 November 2016